STRANGE BEDFELLOWS

Jacinta climbed under the flap of blanket and curled her backside against Michael's belly and thighs. She was icy from the watch. He put his arm around her to pull her closer so that he could warm her, found her forearms crossed stiffly over her breasts. He curled his fingers around her shoulder. "How *did* you get in the Corps?" he whispered. "And how mad is your daddy going to be when he finds out we shared a blanket?"

"My father's dead," she said. "If he were alive, he would have understood. But it's not a detail I'd put in my report. . . ."

ICEMAN

CYNTHIA FELICE

ACE BOOKS, NEW YORK

This book is an Ace original edition
and has never been previously published.

ICEMAN

An Ace Book / published by arrangement with
the author

PRINTING HISTORY
Ace edition / November 1991

ISBN: 0-441-18373-5

Ace Books are published by The Berkley Publishing Group,
200 Madison Avenue, New York, New York 10016.
The name "ACE" and the "A" logo
are trademarks belonging to Charter Communications, Inc.

PRINTED IN THE UNITED STATES OF AMERICA

10 9 8 7 6 5 4 3 2 1

CHAPTER
1

Starfarers.

These were Corps of Means starfarers, the ones who made the magic of starlanes work and—as Michael had learned in the three years he'd served in the Corps—not as arrogant as administrators and politicians, which was to say Michael hated them only a little.

It might have been funny if it hadn't been so stupid; the biggest concern the three lieutenants had in the first hour after the little shuttle crash-landed was what to do about the lack of toilets, and Michael had explained to them about walking a little ways from the signal fire and squatting behind rocks and bushes. They debated whether this would be satisfactory for the woman, which amazed Michael at first, for woman or no, she was a Corps ensign, just as he was. The debate ended when Ensign Jacinta Renya gave the lieutenants a disparaging look, then walked briskly toward an outcropping of sandstone and returned safely a few minutes later. The civilian engineer had followed Jacinta's lead, and eventually the three lieutenants had relieved themselves as well.

Michael knew who she was, of course, and had seen her on board *Ship Lisbon*, usually in the gymnasium during required martial arts classes. Sporting varieties of the same

1

were optional, and she never showed up for those, even
though he'd watched her enough to know that she was
good enough to be ranked among the best. They had never
so much as exchanged a word. He might have been tempted
to ask her who had sponsored her, since Lord Rejos's estate
had sponsored *him*, but he had never seen her in the off-duty
lounge, not even once, and of course firefighters, especially
those who were also kettle tenders, did not work with
navigators. He had assumed that Lord Santos's niece had
access to the officers' lounge and was an honored guest
planetside whenever *Ship Lisbon* orbited a Star Council
World, as was befitting a starborn aristocrat. With such
assumptions on his part, her obvious disdain for the other
starfarers' concern here at the crash site piqued his curiosity. She was not like the other starfarers, and yet she was.

They were wary of the fires, all five of them hanging
back from the open flames, fascinated that Michael fed the
fires by putting his hands into the flames. He wasn't sure
if they were struck by what they thought was bravery or
stupidity, or maybe they had decided it was a natural job for
a Corps of Means firefighter. None offered to help, though
as the day cooled into evening, they edged closer to share
the radiant heat. Michael knew it was quite possible that the
only other open fires any of them had seen were the kind
that sent adrenalin ripping through any sane spacer's body
and, at that, probably only at safe distances as a spectator.
He didn't believe he'd ever heard of any fire getting out
of hand in the starfarers' environs. That was because of
the aspects he had begrudgingly learned to admire about
starfarers: They planned for everything. Even fire preven-
tion was built-in. Starfarers used practically incombustible
building materials with heat sensors that were actually an
ingredient as common as sand or plasteel. Extinguishers
were an integral part of almost any structure, and they came
on automatically. Fire control teams, consisting of genetic
rejects like himself, were trained and ready, and usually
bored by their all-drill, no-action lives. The starfarers pre-
paredness was phenomenal.

Well, nearly. Terrorists, a word he'd learned to use instead of patriots, were pretty hard to plan for, but *these* starfarers weren't worrying about terrorists out here in the middle of the Midwest tundra. They weren't even worrying that they were getting cold—yet. Not while they had Michael to build fires for them. It galled him as much as it amused him that these people who had the wherewithal to command the starlanes for two thousand years could also stand on the very earth from which they had sprung and not know how to keep warm.

Again Jacinta surprised him. He hadn't noticed her slip away from the fire, but she came back with her arms loaded with dead branches and a few chunks of shale in her hands. She kneeled to put the heavy load on the kindling Michael had stacked earlier, and he saw that some of the twigs were wedged in her wrist jacks. As he helped her get untangled, he saw that the skin around her jacks was inflamed, and now the tender skin on the inside of her forearms was scratched and bloody, too. He hoped the damage was only superficial; she'd done a good job of setting the shuttle down safely. He knew enough about navigator jacks to realize the inflammation meant the surgical implants were recent, the buds of internal connections to her nervous system still growing inside her arms.

She brushed the debris from her arms, wincing every time she touched the jacks. Before he could ask if she needed help attending to the jacks, she threw some of the chunks of shale into the fire and nearly knocked him off his feet as she dodged the resulting shower of sparks.

"Why'd you do that?" he asked, waving sparks and smoke from his face.

"I didn't know the sparks would fly so far," she said, genuinely horrified.

"No, I mean the rock. Why'd you put it in the fire?"

"It's firestone," she said, then she crossed her arms across her chest and looked at him, her dark eyes sheepish. "At least it looked like firestone. I used to gather them when I was a little girl on Ballendo. My father would burn them out on the beach on chilly nights."

Michael used a branch to nudge the chunk of shale out of the fire. "It's just a rock," he said, looking back at her because it was fun to see her smiling as she laughed at herself and to see such pretty, dark eyes gazing at him. Most starfarers didn't maintain eye contact as long as he did, and often thought him insolent. If Jacinta thought him insolent, she didn't say so.

The civilian engineer brought some frozen willow twigs over to the pile of firewood. "We'll need more to last the night, won't we?" he asked as he added his small offering to the stack.

"Lots more," Michael said.

"Your name is Michael Jivar, isn't it?" And when Michael nodded, he said, "I'm Paul Matson," which was an unexpected introduction. Protocol forbade a lowly ensign like Michael to initiate discussion with a civilian, and usually civilians treated all but high-ranking officers like servants. Paul Matson acknowledged Michael's hesitant nod with a smile and then left, presumably to find more firewood.

Jacinta was warming her hands as she listened to the ranking lieutenant, Louis Angier, agree with Lieutenant Kateu Nogi's suggestion that they start walking to Topeka. She looked as if she wanted to say something, but then the other lieutenant, Johan Schley, suggested they cannibalize parts from the little shuttle to build another radio. As the officers bogged down discussing the merits of each proposal, Jacinta must have come to the same conclusion Michael had earlier, that they were useless in this situation. The Corps didn't waste planetary survival training on officers who would spend their entire careers monitoring brainjar activity in the brainrooms of Corps of Means ships.

"I'll try to find more dead vegetation," she said quietly to Michael, and walked away from the fire.

Michael watched her for a moment. She was trim and tiny like most starfarers, and somehow managed to look elegant as she stepped gingerly over the broken ground. She was no doubt unaccustomed to anything but perfectly flat flooring underfoot; her grip boots, essential in the ship's corridors, weren't serving her well on rock and crunchy tufts of low-growing grass. She was wearing short-sleeved fatigues that were too thin to provide much warmth, and he wondered what she was wearing underneath. At least she had the good sense to do something that would keep her from freezing during the night. Michael was always annoyed with himself when a starfarer earned even his slightest respect. He knew he was better off to think of them only contemptuously, to remember that individual starfarers should not be credited with all that the descendants of the Four Migrations had accomplished since they left Earth, and not to think of them as superior to those they had left behind. Michael always had to remind himself that though their stature was more compact as a result of their genetic manipulation and the men more handsome and the women more beautiful, the genes were the same as his own. His father had taught him so, and he'd confirmed his father's theory with facts in *Ship Lisbon*'s data base.

The same genes, but carefully arranged so that teeth were always white and even, the body perfectly propor-tioned, with little or no tendency to get too fat, because each of them produced enzymes that had been coded for by a number of manipulated genes. They were supposed to be smarter, too, their genes and chromosomes so well mapped and manipulated that adolescent artists and toddler engineers were commonplace among them. Of course, he reminded himself, those same artists and engineers didn't seem able to put the details of living together sufficiently to exist without servants or the technomagic equivalents. Just like now. The three lieutenants were trying to talk through what to do about being stranded on the still-frozen tundra, as if it were nothing more than a cracked brainjar in the ship's brainroom, where there were many reasonable options and alternatives. Here, in the early spring of their native wilderness, they did not know what was reasonable. Their real homes and true histories were light-years away, even though Earth was the cradle of all their civilizations.

They had returned only fifty years ago to find the cradle blanketed with ice that was miles thick and humanity in what starfarers considered an appalling decline. What had given rise eventually to the steady advance of technology on so many of the pioneer worlds two thousand years ago had merely risen and fallen in weakening waves here on Earth. Starfarers had many theories to explain the severity of this divergence, which ranged from the ancient pioneers' accelerating human evolution through genetic manipulation while the same possibilities stagnated on Earth because of legal encumbrances to the depletion of the planet's natural resources that no amount of innovation could overcome. A Consortium had been formed by agreement among the starfarer Council of Worlds to aid Earth's recovery, especially to find ways and means of reversing the ice age into which the Earth had fallen. Unfortunately, the Consortium had not asked Earth if it wanted help—most nations did— nor if the terms of providing such help were agreeable— they weren't. Even so, the Consortium had established itself in a city constructed at the edge of the Hudson Ice Sheet in southern Illinois. Michael had been brought up in awe of starfarers and their technomagic; he'd learned about their arrogance on his own, and felt the effects of their indifference to him and his people. His three years in the Corps had done little to change what he felt.

Then Jacinta and Paul came back with their arms full of crusty-barked branches and shattered his stereotypes of starfarers again. Too often these days he found himself liking one starfarer or another, the oppression his people endured because of them too easily forgotten in the light of day. Sometimes he wished he could live without sleeping, without dreams, without remembering and without knowing what sleep had felt like with a piece of cardboard for a blanket, without remembering and without knowing that another generation of icers would not sleep warmly if Michael forgot his origins. Or his purpose.

Jacinta dumped another load of firewood, startling him. Her forearms were crusted with blood and dirt, the jacks filled with debris that she picked at now. He knew they must hurt, but she didn't complain.

There were clouds gathering on the horizon as the tundra cooled. It was just early enough in the spring for the sunlight to have thawed the top centimeters of permafrost, but in the dark, the vast, treeless plain froze again. Jacinta shivered and stepped tentatively toward the fire. Paul watched Michael for a moment, then stepped right up to the fire, almost immediately revelling in the heat. The lieutenants, apparently finally cold enough or maybe satisfied that since they weren't smelling burning meat it must be safe, edged closer to the flames, too, until finally all of them were huddled around the fire.

The still-serious discussion the lieutenants were having had changed to examining evidence for the crash landing being a planned survival exercise. Johan Schley was pointing out that failure of the fuel controller right after the communication console stopped working and the subsequent discovery that the ever-reliable transponder didn't work either couldn't possibly be a coincidence.

"They damn well better not have put me down in the middle of a military survival test," Paul said to the lieutenants. They looked at him as if they had forgotten he existed. "I'm a civilian."

"You *say* you're a civilian, but maybe you're an observer," Schley said, more to the other two lieutenants than to Paul.

Paul looked irritated. He shook his head. "I'm a civilian engineer. The Consortium employs thousands of us. I am not some kind of military observer."

"Of course he'd have to say that," Schley said to Angier, who frowned thoughtfully and nodded.

"They wouldn't have had to use a civilian as an observer," Nogi said, "and even if I rule out three simultaneous equipment failures as coincidence, I can't rule out sabotage as the cause."

Schley shook his head. "We're not carrying anything of value, remember?" For a moment he looked triumphant, as if especially pleased with his logic. "We've already checked the manifest and all personal belongings. Nothing."

"Terrorists don't need reasons," Nogi said stubbornly. "Their goal is to disrupt the Consortium; they know they can't overthrow it, so they disrupt wherever they can."

Angier was nodding thoughtfully again.

"Some disruption," Michael said, risking a reprimand for addressing the lieutenant without permission. "The furloughs of two no-stripers, a few brainjar jockeys, and an engineer. Terrorists wouldn't bother with the likes of us."

Angier didn't nod again, but he cupped his chin with his fingers and definitely seemed thoughtful, even though this new observation was from a lowly ensign.

Michael tossed a few more branches on the fire. The starfarers pulled their hands away from the resulting sparks. "How long before they start looking for us, pilot?" he asked Jacinta.

She repeated what she had told all of them before they even stepped out of the shuttle, that Cradle Command already knew the little shuttle had not reestablished contact after ionospheric penetration, and that by morning they would begin full search procedures.

"And we're almost a hundred klicks off course, so they won't get around to looking *here* for days," Schley said, remembering the rest of what Jacinta had told them. "The pilot said Topeka was only forty miles away, and there's a Consortium outpost there. I say we start walking. We can be there in less than two days."

Michael watched Angier scratch his chin and nod.

Jacinta shook her head. "This is where we were an hour ago," she muttered.

From his place at the edge of the flames, Michael looked at her. No one else seemed to have heard what she said, and he was sure she knew that. It was almost as if she were talking to herself.

"I'm going to get my duffle and get some more clothes on," she said. "If anyone else had any sense, they'd do the same."

Again only Michael heard her, for the three lieutenants were talking at once, each providing personal estimates on how far they could walk in one day without much food or water. Michael knew Jacinta couldn't walk forty miles in this terrain wearing grip boots, but he also knew these lieutenants wouldn't consult either of them on what they could or could not do. Quietly, he slipped away, following Jacinta to the shuttle in the last light of day.

From the shuttle hatch he watched Jacinta pull on coveralls over the fatigues. They would not be much extra protection against the cold, but there was nothing else in her duffle. It surprised him to see a pilot's duffle as paltry as his own. Even if she was only an ensign, she was a starfarer, and all of them had more possessions than they could ever use in a lifetime, and that he knew for a fact. His fellow kettle tenders always complained about not having enough stowage space.

Jacinta pulled open the emergency supplies storage bulkhead; ten sealed kits were jumbled, whether from the three lieutenants rummaging around when they were trying to inventory nonexistent cargo or because the hard landing had broken them loose, he didn't know. Each contained a blanket, which would help ward off the cold. Jacinta pulled one kit out.

"Toss me one, too," Michael said.

She whirled around, startled to find him standing at the open hatch.

"Make that two," he said. "I'll take one to the engineer."

"Why not bring them all?" Jacinta asked with a thoughtful frown. "Everyone's going to need one."

"Not everyone deserves one," he said. He raised himself with his hands so that he was sitting on the threshold. "Brass slime warming their butts by the fire we built. You want to bring them blankets, go ahead. Not me. Let them figure it out."

Jacinta tossed him two packs, put the third under her arm, and closed the bulkhead.

"Hey, did you take care of your jacks?" Michael asked. "They looked kind of bloody."

Jacinta looked at her wrists. The blood was dried and crusted over the jacks. "It doesn't matter," she said sadly.

"Doesn't matter? I thought those things were a navigator's pride and joy."

"They probably won't let me keep them," she said softly.

"Just because you crash-landed? I should think you'd get a commendation for getting us down safely."

"It was my first solo, and my last flight. The end of my Corps career."

"I still think you'll get a commendation," Michael said, wondering why she looked so sad. It seemed to him that the Corps took advantage of every opportunity to bestow honors on Corpsmen with high-ranking sponsors. It strengthened the complicated military-civilian co-dependency and mutual ineptness.

She almost smiled. "I meant that my contract is up. I have to go home." She shrugged. "At least I soloed. Even if it did end badly. Funny, I don't even know who pulled the strings to arrange the solo."

"I think I do," Michael said.

She looked at him blankly.

"I mean, I think whoever it was will be proud." Michael swung his feet inside the shuttle. "Sit down," he said, reaching for the medical kit. "I'll clean them for you." She hesitated, but finally sat in one of the passenger seats and let him get to work.

The crusted blood fell away easily once liberally soaked with antiseptic. He flushed bits of remaining vegetation. Underneath her skin he could feel the extra skeletal growth that would eventually anchor her when she plugged into the ship's brainroom circuits.

"We should have three signal fires going," Jacinta said, "not just one."

"Yes, I know," Michael said, surprised that she knew. "I didn't think the Corps gave navigators planetary survival lessons."

"They don't," she said, "but I read a manual once anyhow."

"Well, it's just gotten dark, so now is when having three will count for something. But didn't you say that they wouldn't start search patterns until morning? Something about first giving us a chance to get in on our own?"

Jacinta nodded. "Without a specific call for help, and nothing from the transponder picked up by satellite or other shuttles for that matter, they'll just classify us as missing. We could still be in orbit for all they know." She sat quietly for a moment. "I didn't know the Corps gave planetary survival training to firefighters either."

"They don't," Michael said, surprised that she'd bothered to look at his insignia to learn what his duty assignment was. The navigators and pilots he'd seen had only looked at his wrists to see if he wore jacks, and not finding them, had rebuffed him. He twisted a sliver he'd overlooked. "We get trained in how to control power overloads."

"The boiling kettle drill," she said. "I know about those."

"I guess you would if one happened when you were plugged in," he said. "I'll bet it's like driving a bomb."

"It's scary all right. Even the simulations. I can control everything on the ship through the jacks when I'm plugged in, but if the kettles are boiling, all I can do is hope you kettle tenders will be able to get it under control. I always am amazed that you people handle it so well."

"Funny," he said, "I was just beginning to think of *you* people with your odd genes, jacks, and wired brains as human after all. But that comment could only have come from a cyborg." He flushed the wounds again, just as carefully as before, but not as tenderly.

"I only meant that in a real incident, most of you would die," she said quickly.

"No, that's not what you meant. You think kettle tenders are too stupid to know we're going to die. We may not have the intelligence quotient you pilot-navigator-cyborgs have, but let me tell you . . ." He looked up at her and could tell he had her all wrong. She was horrified. He sighed and squirted more antiseptic on the jacks. "It's true. Sometimes we're stupid. And cruel."

Her expression softened, and she almost smiled.

"Do you need a preventive antibiotic?" he asked when he was satisfied that the jacks were clean.

"I don't know enough about the old world environment to be sure one way or the other," Jacinta said. "Is there much chance of infectious bacteria in the vegetation I carried?"

"When in doubt, do," he said firmly.

It was a quote from *Elementary Medicine in Hostile Environments*, a manual most starfaring military were required to know. Jacinta must have recognized it, for she sighed and nodded. Probably another manual she had read in her spare time, quickly synthesized in moments through the jacks, whereas he had spent hours reading it on the vid. Only the ability to recall on demand segregated the very good navigators from the poor ones who needed the brainjar assists. Michael would have wagered that she was one of the good ones.

Michael rubbed a smudge of dirt off the back of her hand, which he had missed with the antiseptic, and the rest of her medical tattoo came clean. He could already read the code to learn which antibiotic to use, but he swabbed halfway up her arm, cleaning her genecode and herald tattoos as well. "Ballendian, eh? Now that's a herald you don't see often on a woman in the Corps," he said as if he had not known who she was. "Now I understand what the lieutenants were worried about. The modesty and delicacy of Ballendian women is legend."

"Didn't anyone ever tell you it was rude to talk about someone's herald?"

"Yeah, but that doesn't often stop me. Besides, it's not the herald people don't want to talk about, especially when they're wearing a long one like that. It's the genecode they'd rather not discuss." He selected antibiotic tabs from the kit that matched the dosage indicated on her medical tattoo, placed one next to each jack, then slapped generous gauzy white pads over tabs and jacks, stretched a web of

medic gel over her wrists, and held them in place while
the gel spread and sealed. He glanced again at her herald in
the seconds it took for the gel to seal. It wasn't an ordinary
Ballendian herald. Their pilot was of the royal house. He
hadn't known that. "I'll bet there's a story behind this,"
he said, rubbing his thumb over the gold crest. "I suppose
you're going back to Ballendo since you're getting out of
the Corps."

Stiffly, Jacinta pulled her wrists out of his hands. "No,"
she said. "My family lives here on Earth."

He should have hated her, but he didn't. He'd probably
lose sleep over *that* contradiction.

"Wasn't your knee bleeding, too?" he asked, and not
even waiting for her to answer, he reached for her cuff.
She jerked away and he looked up in surprise. She had the
look of a terrified animal. "It *is* bleeding," he said, gesturing
to the stain.

"I know," she said, obviously nervous. "You just startled
me when you touched my leg."

"Is that some kind of female Ballendian reaction?"

"You caught me by surprise, that's all," she said, but she
seemed to be blushing.

"Okay, okay," he said. "Just let me look at the knee."
Jacinta extended her leg, and he pulled the cuffs of the
fatigues and coveralls up to her thigh, which was no higher
than necessary but which obviously distressed her, for she
grabbed the cloth he'd rolled, as if to prevent it from
rolling higher. "Nasty," he said, reaching again for the
antiseptic.

While he worked on her knee, he knew she could see the
tattoos on the back of his wrists. She could have looked
when he'd been working on her wrists, but probably she
did what everyone else did, sort of look at them from the
edge of her vision only when she was curious—like now.
His herald had two stripes, one red, one white, each with
five blue stars. Beneath it was the standard medical code
the Corps required, and between the tattoos his genecode
with only a single generation represented.

"Never saw anything like it, did you?" Michael said quietly.

Jacinta glanced up, embarrassed to realize she'd been caught staring.

Michael chuckled and slapped the web over the cleansed wound on her knee. "It's okay, Jacinta. Why would they put them right on the wrist if people really weren't supposed to look?" He pressed the web firmly on her knee. "I'm a 'Merican," he said. "No, excuse me. I'm an American. I was a 'Merican, for sixteen years, but then I joined the Corps and they taught me to say American."

"An Earthling?" she said. "An old world native in the Corps?"

He took his hand away from her knee, snapped the kit shut, nodding, even though, like most starfarers, she'd misused the term native. "And you *know* there's a story behind that," he said, smiling because, aside from being surprised, Jacinta looked pleased, and somehow that pleased him. He stowed the kit and backed toward the hatch, scooping up the two survival kits, then he jumped lightly to the ground. "Come on," he said. "Let's go back to the fire and get warm while I tell you how a 'Merican iceman came to be in the Corps of Means."

She rolled down her pants leg and scrambled to jump out after him. The sun was so far below the horizon now that there was only the faintest hint of pink at the edge of the ice sheet. The rest of it looked like a black wall. "And I suppose I'm to tell you how a Ballendian woman came to be in the Corps of Means?" she said, catching up to him.

"It's either that or listen to the brass slime stand around talking out of their assholes. Take your pick, Ensign Renya."

The civilian engineer had kept the fire going, and was crouched as close to the flames as Michael had been earlier. The three officers were still huddled in discussion, but when they saw Michael break out the silvery blanket from his kit and realized that they had none, they encouraged each other to go back to the shuttle to fetch more kits. Michael was surprised they hadn't ordered him back, but perhaps they were decent enough to want to give some appearance of self-sufficiency.

"Ensign Renya and I are going to tent our blankets to catch the heat from the fires," Michael said to the engineer. "Do you want to join us?"

Jacinta gave the briefest *we are?* look before apparently deciding it was for the best and starting to help him. The engineer, after a moment's assessment of how Michael was rigging his and Jacinta's blankets and a disparaging look into the darkness where the three officers had disappeared, nodded and pulled his blanket from the kit. With nothing more than sticks to prop the blankets up, and by sitting on a flap, they were warmed in minutes by trapped, radiant heat.

"We'll be fine if the wind doesn't come from the glacier," the engineer said. Then he shook his head. "You realize not one of those officers has any idea of what to do, don't you?"

"What did you expect from brainjar tenders?" Michael said easily. "As long as they spend all their time planning what to do just in case, we'll be fine, 'cause that will leave Ensign Renya and me free to do what we need to do just in time."

"Just in time for what?" the engineer asked, obviously not amused by Michael's irreverence.

Michael shrugged. "Whatever. They aren't going to do anything before dawn."

"And then?"

"How the hell would I know?" Michael said. "I'm nothing but an ensign, and you can be sure they won't ask for my opinion."

"Which means they're not going to have the benefit of the second most well-informed opinion in the group," Jacinta said with a sigh.

"Second best?" Michael said, bristling.

Jacinta laughed. "You may be the only native Earthling around, but they've already had the best information from me, which was that given the circumstances it will take the searchers between twenty-four and a hundred hours to find us and that as long as some great whites don't come looking for a meal, we should stay put. We're in good physical condition and more likely to stay that way if we wait. We could injure ourselves if we try to walk around in this god-forsaken wilderness and encounter who knows what."

Michael nodded. "I know what, and I agree. And no, there are no great whites around here. Wolves, caribou, and musk-oxen, but none of them will come near the fire."

"Great whites?" the engineer asked.

"Bears. Five-hundred-kilo carnivores. They aren't much 'fraid of fires," Michael said. "They mostly live at the edge of The Cold, but a thousand miles east. They say they don't range as far as Illinois, let alone Kansas."

"Do you know that for a fact?" the engineer asked sharply.

"No," Michael said. He moved the stick that supported the edge of his blanket so that some of the trapped heat would circulate more freely behind him. "I've never been to Kansas before. Been to Whitney Planet and Dolphinia, but never went more than fifty klicks from Cradle City in Illinois before I joined the Corps."

The engineer was surprised. "You seem like a nice kid," he said.

"You mean, for a Neanderthal?" Michael snapped, unable to restrain himself.

"I mean, you seem like a nice kid," the engineer said calmly. He looked up to meet Michael's glare. "Smart enough to get by in a tough situation despite being out-ranked by three dolts who call themselves officers, not to mention having a civilian, who knows absolutely nothing about the old world, all depending on you."

Michael broke eye contact and stared into the fire. He felt hot and ashamed, yet knew he shouldn't. For every starfarer like Paul Matson, he knew there were ten arrogant banties determined to rule Earth.

The officers came back with all seven remaining survival kits. They erected a heat trap on the other side of the signal fires with three of the blankets and spread another to sit on, then they inventoried the food packs, including what had been in the kits Michael and Jacinta had brought back to the fire. They also announced two-hour watches through the night, starting with lowest-ranking Michael and skipping the civilian entirely. Then they began discussing how to apportion the three remaining blankets between the two heat traps.

"I'll take one for the watch," Michael said, taking one blanket before they were quite sure what was happening. "The sleepers can share." He passed the blanket to Jacinta and the engineer.

The engineer looked at Jacinta questioningly. He had not studied her herald, but just like the lieutenants, he'd probably been aware of her Ballendian herald early on. What Michael was suggesting would be completely unacceptable if Jacinta had been a civilian Ballendian, and he was apparently uncertain what her wearing a Corps uniform brought to the situation.

"Corps survival laws prevail," Jacinta said to him, "not the bloodlaws."

"If you're sure," he said, still uneasy.

"She's sure," Michael said when Jacinta hesitated.

Later, when her watch was over, Jacinta started to curl up between the fire and the sleeping engineer with just a flap of the blanket to cover her. Michael sat up.

"Come here," he whispered, raising the front flap of the blanket that had covered his backside. "If I'm not between you two, they'll wake me up when they run out of firewood, and we're sure to before dawn. Maybe they won't risk waking you or the civilian."

"They're not Ballendians," she said.

"No, but they know Ballendians run the Consortium, and two of them are Constantinians, who must understand Ballendian bloodlaws. They won't risk your daddy or brother claiming a blood insult for dragging you out of bed."

Still she hesitated.

"Come on," he urged, "you know the civilian is nervous about it anyway."

Jacinta relented. She climbed under the flap of blanket and curled her backside against Michael's belly and thighs. She was icy from the watch. He put his arm around her to pull her closer so that he could warm her, found her forearms crossed stiffly over her breasts. He curled his fingers around her shoulder. "How *did* you get in the Corps?" he whispered. "And how mad is your daddy going to be when he finds out we shared a blanket?"

"My father's dead," she said. "If he were alive, he would have understood. But it's not a detail I'd put in my report, which my uncle could read if he wanted to. He runs the Consortium, and he wouldn't understand."

So saying, she snuggled deeper into his arms. Her hair smelled smoky. Michael still wasn't sure if she thought him brave or stupid, but he didn't much care right now either. He would sleep no more tonight. Nor would any of the others sleep through until dawn.

CHAPTER
2

"Ge' 'p."

Jacinta felt Michael's arm tighten across her chest. She was cold; the fires had gone out, and now one of the officers was waking her up to go find firewood. Michael's ploy hadn't worked, she thought groggily.

Someone ripped the blanket off. Now she was really cold—and angry. Even in the first weeks of training, the officers hadn't used such juvenile tactics. She sat bolt upright, intending to give the offending lieutenant a scathing look, and gasped. She was staring down the barrel of a gun. Not a clean-looking stunner, but a lethal-looking projectile launcher. Michael sat up right behind her, wordless.

The man holding the gun was crouched nervously in the ashes of the fire. He was a big man, dark-haired and bearded and wearing dark, bulky clothing, unquestionably a native Earthling. His pale eyes looked cold in the moonlight. He waved the gun. "Ge' 'p," he said again.

"Get up," Michael whispered urgently. "Stand."

As she stood up, she saw Michael shake Paul Matson, cautioning him as he came awake. On the other side of the ashes was another dark-clad man holding a gun to Lieutenant Angier's head. The young lieutenant looked frightened.

"W' zit?" The gunman pressed the barrel against Lieutenant Angier's temple. "W' za gol'?"

"They killed Nogi and Schley," Angier said through almost clenched teeth. He gestured with his eyes, and Jacinta saw Lieutenant Nogi sprawled on the frozen ground near some rocks. She hadn't been able to see that far last night; dully, she realized that dawn was breaking.

Once Michael and the engineer were on their feet, the light-eyed gunman ripped down the silvery tent, scattering the blankets. "N'ing," he said in disgust.

"W' za gol'?" the other gunman shouted in Lieutenant Angier's ear.

The lieutenant cringed. "I don't know what you want," he managed to say.

The gunman drew back and slapped the lieutenant in the face with the gun. The lieutenant cried out as blood spurted from his nose. "Te" m'," the gunman shouted, and hit him again.

Jacinta stared, horrified and frozen with fear. She had no idea what these people wanted or why they had murdered the other two lieutenants, but she was already certain they were going to kill her even if she didn't know. Beside her, the engineer flinched as the gunman kicked the lieutenant and shouted something unintelligible.

"Do you understand them?" the engineer managed to ask Michael.

"They want gold," Michael whispered.

"Tell them we don't have any," the engineer said frantically.

"They aren't going to believe me; all starfarers have gold."

"Sh'p," the light-eyed gunman said. He cracked Michael across the face with his gun hand, and Michael fell.

"No gold," the engineer said, his hands raised to show empty palms. "No—wait! I have a gold-cased . . ." He started fumbling at the little metallic case hitched to his belt, but before he could finish what he was saying, the light-eyed gunman pointed the gun and shot the engineer in the head.

Jacinta muffled her scream behind her hands as the engineer crumpled, a hole in his forehead the size of her fist. She had never even imagined savagery of this magnitude could happen, and the panic rising in her was like none she'd ever known.

The gunman leveled the gun at Jacinta, then swung it around to Michael, who still lay on the ground.

"Don't move," Michael said.

She hadn't planned to move. She wasn't even sure she would if she could. Dear god, this was no time to fall into a panic.

The gunman stepped over to the fallen engineer to open the case on his belt and pulled out a gold-inlaid cipher unit. He put it in the pocket of his big coat and went through the rest of the engineer's clothes. He pocketed a few coins, then turned to the other gunman. "N' gun," he said. "N' gol'."

"We aren't even armed," the lieutenant said, "and we're not carrying any gold. It was a passenger shuttle, and we made a forced landing."

"Gol'?" the bigger gunman said, leaning over the lieutenant, threatening to hit him again.

"No gold," Jacinta said before the man could swing again. He looked up at her. "No gold," she repeated, feeling all the more frightened because he was looking at her. She wanted to explain that passenger shuttles never carried precious cargo, but she'd already seen that they weren't understanding the lieutenant any more than they had the engineer. She had to keep it simple. "No gold," she said again.

"Te" m', bitch," the gunman said savagely. He stood up and took a step toward her. "Te" m' wh'z!"

Michael stood up. "Ain' n' gol'," he said. "Lady try'n tuh te" yuh, plane 'z'n' car'n gol'."

The first gunman scowled at Michael. "Don't trus' n' beento," he said to the other man.

"Te" n tru'," Michael said simply. "Lady'z, too. 'N' t' brass. Ain' got 'ny gol'."

Jacinta bit her lip. She could almost understand when Michael was speaking, but she could tell that the gunman didn't believe him any more than he had believed the lieutenant.

"Te" m', beento, 'n' yuh live. Don't talk now, 'n' yuh die," the light-eyed gunman said. He stepped up to Jacinta, and put his gun to her head. "Meyb' yuh don' bli'v' m'?"

"Bli'v' yuh, man, b' don' ha' gol'," Michael said quickly.

"Tell him passenger shuttles don't have gold on them," the lieutenant said. "Make him understand that we crashed."

"Don' lis'n brass, beento. Yer ass, n'z," the big gunman said.

"Stop talking," Michael said sharply to the lieutenant. "He doesn't understand everything you say, and he thinks you're trying to stop me from telling him where the gold is." Michael faced the light-eyed gunman again and brought his hand up in a helpless gesture. "Banty'z jus' tr'n say same'z m'. Ain' n' gol'."

Jacinta felt the gunman press the barrel against her cheek. The icy metal felt like fire. "Te", 'r I shoot'r," he said. Jacinta closed her eyes, certain a projectile was about to blow her brains out. She heard the shot, but felt nothing. Amazing. No pain. She could even feel her muscles clench. They'd probably give out. She heard something fall, and her eyes fluttered open. The lieutenant had keeled into the ashes. Michael was staring.

"Sh'z nex'," the light-eyed gunman said.

" 'Kay 'kay," Michael said suddenly. "I' sho' yuh." He started to walk toward the shuttle. "Comin'?" he said to the light-eyed gunman.

"Wa'cha lady," and the gunman shoved her aside.

The other gunman considered a moment, then let his companion go with Michael. "S'down," he said to Jacinta. "Gimme w'z'n yer pock'ts," he added.

"What?" she said, although now she thought she understood him. She was also certain Michael was stalling for time, and she could think of nothing better to do than to follow his lead. Then she realized the remaining gunman was leering at her, and she wasn't at all sure that all he wanted her to do was to empty her pockets and sit down. She made a puzzled gesture, and he shook his head.

"Be ni'z 'n' mebbe yuh live," he said. He licked his lips, slowly, suggestively.

Jacinta glared at him, and he laughed.

"Like 'm w'spunk," he said.

"I'd die first," she said, which made him laugh even more. As she watched him adjust his crotch, she tried to look contemptuous. Inwardly, she was sure that if he took one step toward her, she'd collapse in terror. Maybe when Michael and the other gunman returned without any gold, they'd be so angry they'd just shoot them both and be done with it. She was sure it would be worse if they decided to take all their frustration out on her. She couldn't help thinking that if their bodies were ever recovered and a full report supplied to Uncle Ramon on how she died, he would silently let the Corps arrange for the disposal of her tainted remains. The thought enraged her.

I won't die, she thought fiercely. I'll jump across those ashes and kick the gun out of his hand. She nearly threw herself into the thought, but remembered from hand-to-hand exercises what she wanted to do was not easy. At least, not faster than the big man could pull the trigger. She had to be closer. Suddenly she knew how to accomplish that.

"All right," she said, her voice trembling. "Before your friend comes back."

"Huh?" said the gunman, puzzled.

"Why wait? He'll just want me first. Come on," she said. But he was frowning at her, as if she did not understand. Fingers trembling, she started to open her coveralls. He watched her placidly for a moment. "Don't tell me you still don't understand," she muttered. But when she opened the fatigues, he smiled.

" 'S bettuh," he said, and sat on a rock, leveling the gun at her.

She took a tentative step toward him, tugging at the shoulders. She had underwear on, and he gestured upward with the gun. He wanted everything off, but she knew she'd be dead or he'd be disarmed before it came to that. Not even to save her life could she completely disrobe before any man, let alone a Neanderthal. She took her time peeling back first the coveralls, and then the fatigues. The gunman started fumbling with his pants, and suddenly she was petrified that he'd get them open. There was the most god-awful look of anticipation on his face, and when the shot rang out, it didn't change, except that now he seemed to have another open mouth where his forehead should be.

The gunman's arms slumped, the weapon dropped to the ground, but he sat with his pants half-open, as if pinned by the bullet that had gone through his forehead.

"It's okay," she heard Michael say from behind her. He stepped up to look at the gunman, pushed him over. "The other one's dead, too."

Jacinta couldn't speak. It had never occurred to her that Michael might be able to disarm and dispatch the other gunman, let alone kill this one in the nick of time.

Michael tucked the gun in his belt and turned around. He looked at her, her fatigues and coveralls hanging from her waist, the thin chemise covering her breasts. He stared with a look of faintly amused incredulity. Instinctively, she covered her chemise with her arms.

"I had to get closer to take the gun away," she stammered as she turned her back to him to shove her arm into a sleeve. The other sleeve escaped her. She was badly shaken, almost as much from what Michael might be thinking as from nearly losing her life. She couldn't get her arm into the sleeve.

Then she felt Michael grab the fatigues and shove her arm into the sleeve. He pulled the coveralls up, too, and she realized he was grinning. "You were going to take the gun away from him?" he said.

She wanted to slap the smile off his face. Instead, she knocked his hands away with her forearms, and fastened the front of the fatigues and the coveralls. "What the hell did you think I was going to do?" she said. "Lay down with an iceman?"

"Don't get angry," he said. "You never stood up to those lieutenants like a highborn, so I sure didn't expect any help from you."

"Did you think I was just going to stand here and let them kill me?"

"Pretty much," he said. "You're a Ballendian lady."

"Who wears a Corps uniform," she said fiercely. "And navigational jacks, too. You should have known better."

"I'll remember that next time," he said sincerely, and maybe with some admiration, but still grinning. "Well, since I don't need to treat you like a lady, I guess you can help me drag these corpses back to the shuttle. Don't want the blood attracting wolves."

"My god," she said, looking at the engineer's body. "How could this have happened so quickly? The sun's barely up, and four good people are dead."

"Well, one, anyhow," Michael said, "and three who were useless, not to mention the two who needed killing."

"How did you . . ."

"Cut his throat. Took his gun, and came back to get you. Saw a clear shot and took it."

He picked up a blanket and threw it over the lieutenant, then grabbed up the feet and started dragging the corpse away. His face was expressionless.

Jacinta picked up one of the blankets; her fingers were trembling, and she couldn't get the engineer's corpse covered. Michael came to help her. "Where's Lieutenant Schley?" she said, trying to pick up another blanket. She felt numb, but was determined to do what needed to be done.

"Back behind those rocks. I guess he was taking a piss when they got him. Nogi must have heard something, but they got him right over there. Probably surprised Angier in his sleep, just like they did us."

He didn't cover the gunmen; just picked up the feet of the closest one and started to drag him away. Jacinta wanted to cry. He could have been dragging a log for all the regret he showed. Then she was crying, bitterly trying not to, fumbling with just trying to pick up another blanket so she could cover the other lieutenants.

"I'll do it," Michael said, taking the slippery blanket away from her.

"How can you be this way?" she said, truly amazed and distressed because he did not even seem shaken. "Don't you have feelings? Weren't you frightened? Aren't you horrified?"

She could see him tense. Then he scooped up another blanket and walked away. Doggedly, Jacinta pulled the other gunman away from the campfires, angry and somehow still frightened tears streamed down her face as she struggled toward the shuttle. She willed them to stop by pulling harder on the corpse. She dropped it a few feet away from the other gunman, stood staring at them a moment. For the first time she noticed that they were young, the one barely bearded, and somehow they looked innocent. Amazed that such a thought could even cross her mind after what they'd done, she turned away.

Back at the campfire, she found Michael scattering ashes. He'd piled up the rest of the blankets, and moved their camp about twenty feet away from the blood-soaked ground. He even had a few dried sticks of firewood. He saw her coming, and walked away, as if he didn't want to be around her. She sat down near the handful of sticks, and tried to light them with her torch, but her fingers were trembling so badly she couldn't keep the element steady. She had to calm herself. She breathed deeply; the sharp, cold air didn't seem to go down. She sat there staring at the sticks that wouldn't burn.

Michael dumped another armload of firewood, startling her. She had no idea how long she had been staring, unable to think or get hold of herself.

"Want me to start it?" he asked.

"What?"

"The fire." He took one look at her and pulled his own torch out. The fire blazed almost instantly. "Jacinta, you can't let it get to you like this," he said.

"You mean, not if I'm Corps?" she said bitterly, because she wasn't Corps anymore. She was nothing more than a Ballendian woman now, and by the strictest interpretation a disgraced one.

"Not if you're a survivor," he said. "Corps or any other kind."

"How can you not feel it?"

"I didn't say I didn't feel it," he said. "Just don't let it get to you."

"Don't worry," she said. "I won't cry anymore."

"I didn't say don't cry," he said. "You'd better let that out, if you're wanting to."

Fiercely, she shook her head, but tears leaked out again. This time there was no controlling them, and as she buried her face in her hands, she felt Michael's arms around her. Oh, no, she thought. I can't break down in front of this kettle tender. But she couldn't stop, and though she tried to tear herself away from him, she couldn't do that either. "Don't tell," she sobbed. "Don't tell them what I did. Don't tell them I took my clothes off."

"I won't tell anyone," he said, pulling her closer, cradling her against his chest.

She felt a fool, she felt like a child, but she clung to his chest, and she cried.

Late in the morning, Michael convinced Jacinta that they should search for more firewood, even though he'd already found enough to last another night. For all her Corps training, he could see she had been badly shaken. He still wasn't quite sure if the brutality she'd witnessed had traumatized her or if she'd shocked herself with her own will to live by starting to take off her clothes for the gunman. But she was traumatized, there was no denying that. He hoped that a bit a physical activity would help her regain control. She'd been following him for an hour now, obedient about picking up willow and birch twigs they found where the lie of the land broke the winds and allowed the stunted trees to grow, but she was listless. Now they'd topped a rise, from where they could actually see the glacier terminus. They were closer than he thought.

"It almost looks like snow-capped mountains," she said, speaking for the first time. "Can we go closer?"

"If you're willing to keep walking," he said.

She nodded.

He stopped pretending to look for well-drained sites where the willow and birches flourished and took the most direct route. By the time they reached the edge of the glacier, the sun was overhead, and it was actually quite warm. True spring was breaking at last, and the waters were gushing from the glacier in slush-filled rivulets. In a few weeks, the whole plain would be flooded.

Not fifty yards from where the glacier towered over them, he selected some rocks well above the meltwater streams and dumped the twigs out of the blanket he was using as a makeshift sack so they could sit on it. Both of them were sweating and ready to rest. He handed her a foodstick, and was gratified when she peeled it and started eating.

"I want to touch it before we go," she said.

"Touch what—the glacier?"

"Yes. For years I saw it through the wind-keeps in my uncle's castle, but I never got to see it this close. I may never get another chance to actually touch it."

Michael was not really interested in getting much closer. He'd been willing to walk long enough and far enough for her body to start pumping endorphins instead of adrenalin, but since that had started happening, more walking, especially away from the shuttle and camp, seemed a waste of effort. He did not number the glacier among things about Earth that he had missed while he was serving on *Ship Lisbon*.

She looked longingly at the glacier, but she didn't argue with him. Despite his feeling lazy, he wasn't sure he liked her easy agreement. He could tell she was disappointed. He thought about it for a moment. He knew most Cradle City starborn never went much beyond the winter playgrounds they carved out of the ice and snow near the terminus so they could ski, ice skate, and toboggan in comfort. But even that would be denied to Ballendian females, as were most sports.

"Look, if you really want to go, let's go," he said, starting to get up.

"Not if you don't want to," she said.

"Well, I don't, but . . ." Michael was still preparing to leave, but she wouldn't get up.

"It's all right," she said, staying seated. "We'll do as you wish."

They sat silently for a while, warm in the sunshine. In the distance, Michael could see musk-oxen walking in a line to drink from the meltwater. He pointed them out to Jacinta, then pulled the field glasses from his pack so she could see them better. She accepted the glasses and watched them intently as they continued to come closer.

"They're very big," she said, "and still coming our way."

"They don't fear anything, not even men with guns. Those men were probably out looking for this band when they found us."

"My uncle uses rifles to hunt," Jacinta said. "Not handguns."

Michael shrugged. "Those guys weren't hunters; they're poachers. Icemen use anything they can get their hands on including handguns, which are fine for oxen. The oxen stand their ground when threatened, form a circle with the calves in the middle. Easy head shots."

"Do they eat them?" Jacinta asked with obvious revulsion.

Michael nodded. "The meat is good. The under-wool makes the softest shirts. That's why they're protected." He looked at her. "Starfarer protection. The under-wool is even finer than Constantinian cashmir goat's wool, and you get pounds of quivat off a musk-ox, where you get only ounces from a goat. The yarn is planet Earth's sole export, did you know that?"

"No, I didn't know," she said.

"I'm surprised," he said. "Your uncle buys up most of the hunting passes every year."

"Oh," she said, "you know who my uncle is."

"Unless the head of the Consortium has changed since I was last home, yes, I know who Lord Ramon Santos is."

"He is still the head. You don't approve of him, do you?"

"There isn't an iceman who does."

"It may be that there would be no musk-ox alive if he did not protect them."

"Do you believe that?"

"I'd like to," she said, but she looked very troubled. Somehow Michael didn't think it had anything to do with musk-ox.

"Don't think about them anymore," he said.

She didn't misunderstand. "I can't help it. They were just t
ying to feed their families, weren't they."

Michael shook his head. "Not these," he said. "Ordinary poachers would have given us wide berth. These are the kind who even icemen hate."

"They called you something," she said. "It sounded like . . . beento?"

Michael laughed. "Yeah, been to Cradle City, been to the stars. It's about as derogatory a name as you can call an iceman, even worse then Neanderthal. It assumes you've given up all the ways of old Earth."

"But you haven't, have you?"

"I don't know. Earth is my home, I love it," Michael said. "I think highly of the Corps of Means. They've taught me a great deal."

"Honor?"

"Leave it to a starborn to assume that an iceman wouldn't know anything about honor unless he learned it from the Corps of Means," Michael said, bristling.

"I only wanted to know if you understood Ballendian honor codes," she said hastily. "Each world has variations of what honor means, and it's treated with varying importance no matter where you go. On Ballendo, honor comes before law."

"And bloodlaws come before civil law, so what does that have to do with my being a beento or an iceman or anything else in the universe that could possibly relate to you and me sitting on a rock in the middle of the tundra?"

She frowned. "Michael, you must not tell them what I did. Not in your report. Not to anyone. Never. My life is in your hands."

"Pardon?"

"I don't think you understand how serious this is for me. My uncle would never forgive me if he knew I had undressed in front of that man." She looked at him, eyes wide. "Nor you either, for seeing me that way."

Michael would have laughed but for the fear that wouldn't leave her eyes. "I can't believe your kinsmen wouldn't understand the grave circumstances we were in. They should be proud of you. Besides, you're in the Corps of Means. They may be Ballendian, but they cannot be practicing the bloodlaws all that strictly if they agreed to let you join the Corps."

"The circumstances of my going to the Corps are very unusual. I have the right genes for navigation jacks."

"I guessed that much. They're pretty rare, but having them doesn't mean they conscript you." He laughed. "They don't even do that to Neanderthals."

"Stop laughing at me," she said sharply. "Damn. How can I make you understand? It would be one thing for my uncle just to turn his back on me, and if I thought for one second that that's all that would happen, I would beg you to tell them that man raped me."

"What?" Now Michael was really confused.

"I might be able to stay in the Corps if that was all that would happen. I could reenlist. God knows the Corps doesn't care about my virtue; they only care about the jacks. But it's a matter of honor for my uncle. *His* honor more than mine. And he won't let it pass. What I did was dishonorable, unforgivable."

"No one even saw your . . . anything," Michael couldn't help protesting. "You had that white thing covering you."

"Yes, but I was disrobing," she said.

"Under force," Michael said. "If not physical force, certainly understandable duress."

"No," she protested. "I'm Ballendian. The bloodlaws say I should have been willing to die before submitting like that. My uncle won't understand. If he doesn't kill me, he *will* shut me away for having dishonored him. His honor is everything."

"But in the Corps . . ."

"No dispensation for being in the Corps of Means," she said, cutting him off frantically. "Not from the modesty laws, not from anything. It is possible to obey Corps rules without violating Ballendian bloodlaws. I *know*. I've done it for several years. And he knows it, too, because he gets every report in the brainjars that mention my name. That's part of the deal you were wondering about when you asked how a Ballendian lady came to be in the Corps of Means. With the single exception of when I was under direct orders, I had to behave like a Ballendian lady would behave. My officers were handpicked, Constantinians mostly, who could be trusted not to put me in compromising situations while I was on duty just to test their authority or anything like that. But your report could end all that. His honor and his family's honor are inseparable."

"It must have been difficult for you," he said, realizing he believed her. "What did you do in off hours? Stay in your cubey?"

"Yes."

"For years?"

"Yes."

"My god!" Even Michael, who had not been accepted well because of who he was, had not been so complete a recluse that he didn't frequent the commons and entertainments on *Ship Lisbon*, even though he had to do it alone. Of course, he had not wanted his records to call any special attention to his behavior, especially not behavior that was undesirable. She, on the other hand, must have preferred the unofficial black mark of reclusiveness in favor of Ballendian honor, which he knew for a woman of her station included proper escorts on all occasions. He had assumed she would not be subject to the bloodlaws at all while she was in the Corps. Paul Matson's caution had been closer to the mark. "Why would your family subject you to such rigors?" he couldn't help asking.

"When the Fringe World Wars started, there was a shortage of navigators. In plain truth, my uncle saw an opportunity to take control of the Consortium when so many other qualified leaders left Earth to support the war effort. It was a show of support for him to stay behind and to insist that his entire family be crosschecked for navigator genes. I was the only one who qualified."

"So he sent you?"

"Not at first. No one questioned him; girls don't go to war. But I begged him and explained to him how my going wouldn't disgrace him. Even so, I don't think that's what changed his mind," she said, looking thoughtful for a moment. "More likely it was his unpopularity with the rest of the Consortium. If only I had had my jacks then . . ." She shook her head. "My cousin told me that my uncle had been advised by his strategic analysts to offer me, that it would solidify his position. I don't know if sending me really swayed enough opinions for him to take control, but he became the head of the Consortium shortly after he announced that he'd let me go. Then there was a delay while he selected a sponsor, but finally even that was done. The Corps was desperate enough to take me for three years rather than the five they generally demand of navigators." She rubbed one of her jacks. "He'll insist that I wear long sleeves until they can be removed."

"And you'll comply?"

"What choice do I have?" she asked him. "I hate going back. I kept praying he'd extend my contract. I even asked my commander to intercede with him on my behalf. My uncle said he'd forgive me for doing that if I came home

promptly and didn't force him to expose my impertinence
by imposing the contract he has with the Corps for my
services in the courts."

"The Corps won't back you even though you want to
stay?"

"No. They can't. I checked that out on my own by
using my jacks. Every law brainjar I could access told
me the same thing. The contract is good. The Corps recog-
nizes each homeworld's sovereignty of individual rights. A
Ballendian woman cannot resign or reenlist if the male who
holds her papers doesn't agree to let her." She looked at him
solemnly. "Michael, it's bad enough that I am out here in
this wilderness alone with you, but it's forgivable because
circumstances are clearly out of my control and because
I have not ever given anyone cause to doubt my virtue.
But taking off my clothes . . ." She was blushing furiously.
"That was within my control. I could have chosen to die,
and received an honorable burial. I beg you not to tell what
really happened in your report."

He didn't care that he would have to lie in his report, but
he wondered how much risk he'd be taking in trusting her
to lie, too. If she recanted whatever lies they concocted,
he could be discharged for falsifying a report, a mark he'd
carry even on civilian records, which would effectively
ban him from all dealings with starfarers. But he believed
Jacinta when she said her uncle's honor was more important
to him than her life; Ballendian bloodlaws were so fierce in
their demands that even other starfarers were cautious in
their dealings with Ballendians. Michael knew he should
be doubly cautious. But she kept looking at him, her eyes
dilated and dark.

"I guess if I were that cautious, I wouldn't be here," he
finally said.

"What do you mean?" she said.

"Never mind. I'll do what you ask, but on two conditions."

"Conditions?" she said, warily. "What kind of conditions?"

"First, that you never beg me again for anything, and if you do ask me for anything you do it without first patronizing with stupid remarks like not minding that we don't go to the glacier. I'm not a Ballendian man, and I just get confused when you do something like that."

"And the second condition?" she said.

"That you get me an invitation to stay in your uncle's castle for a while."

"What?" She was startled by his request, but the dread in her face lifted immediately. "If you're confused by Ballendian behavior, why would you want to stay in one of their homes and be around them?"

"Because just as you have lived within sight of the glacier but never touched it, I have seen Cradle City looking like a jewel above the tiaga and have never been in it." He laughed. "Despite my being a beento, Cradle City I have not been to."

She stared at him for a full minute. "Your first condition I can meet," she said. "I learned a lot in the Corps. Even though I didn't always dare to use it, I've always wanted to. I used to think about what it would be like to speak my mind, and sometimes I even did it." She smiled shyly but triumphantly. "But I cannot ask my uncle's hospitality for you. It would be unseemly."

"Oh," he said, disappointed.

"There is a way," she said, going on rapidly, almost breathlessly. "You saved my life. My uncle is in your debt whether he likes it or not. He'll offer you rewards of some kind, and if you refuse them, he'll continue to be in your debt. He's sure to believe you've refused out of ignorance, but if you say something like your needing nothing more than a place to stay while you're on furlough, he's sure to offer you his hospitality himself. He won't want you to leave with a blood-debt still owed, because he'd be afraid you'd learn its value and call it in when he least expects it."

"I know how valuable a blood-debt is," he said. "I'm in the Corps because of a blood-debt owed to my father."

"I was wondering how a native Earthling got in," she said. "I've always heard the icers' genetic proclivities are not adequate for Corps service."

"You've heard lies," he said. "Our genealogy and chromosomal patterns are not as well mapped as yours, but our brains function quite well."

"Do you believe your children might be navigators?" she asked.

He thought she was being deliberately playful with the subject matter in some kind of attempt to keep her agreement not to patronize him. But it was not something he cared to joke about. The pain ran too deep. "I believe I *am* a navigator," he said, "and you people don't have the wherewithal to know it." He got up and pulled the blanket out from under her. "Come on. Let's go touch the glacier."

CHAPTER
3

An event investigator had taken charge of Jacinta and Michael the moment the rescue craft had landed on the military side of the Port Authority holdings. He'd been on the tarmac waiting for them, a tall Constantinian man, almost as tall as Michael, and very grim-looking. Jacinta supposed the scowl had to do with his task of first understanding the events that had lead to four starborn men dying at the hands of a couple of lowly icers, and then disposing of the matter in a fashion that would be satisfactory to his Consortium superiors. But Jacinta couldn't help worrying that he might be frowning at her. He must have done some investigating while the rescue craft was on the way; he greeted her as Lady Jacinta, not Ensign Renya, and barely gave her time to drop her duffle before shunting her off to the biomechanical lab for a physical examination. She was not permitted so much as a dry shower, and she knew why. She might be in a Corps of Means facility, but she was no longer in its jurisdiction. She was her uncle's niece once again, not Ensign Renya.

The procedure was noninvasive and considered painless, but those were only physical descriptions. It was tedious and humiliating to lie there, unable to move, while icy calipers touched even the most intimate parts of the body, which was why almost everyone opted for sedation that left them both amnesiac and refreshed. Jacinta could never bring herself to want to pretend the examination had never happened. That would be too easy, and just the beginning of letting herself forget what was real, perhaps even forgetting the true reason she was having this examination even before a thorough event investigation took place, even before being permitted to bathe. She didn't believe that the event investigator had decided this on his own. He had to have already contacted her uncle, who she knew would not be satisfied to hear that she was alive and appeared to be unharmed. He would insist on proof, as was his right as her guardian. Damn, no one should have that kind of power over another person. But here she was, and now it was a matter of record that Lady Jacinta Renya was still a virgin, even after three years in the Corps of Means and three nights on the tundra of Earth alone with nonBallendian men and even some knaves. That ought to satisfy her uncle, but it infuriated Jacinta. After three years of the comparatively free life as a navigator in the Corps of Means, how could she ever bring herself to conform again to the role of a Ballendian woman?

She'd done a poor job of preparing herself. On the one hand, spending half her considerable spare time researching every possible angle for staying in the Corps, everything from finding a way to break the contract her uncle had with the Corps for her three years of service to getting it extended. It had been a waste of time, although she was now considered an expert in Corps/civilian service contracts. Yet, even while she'd been trying to find the means to escape the contract's conclusion, she'd assumed the safest possible posture during her Corps years in preparation for returning to her uncle's domain. With the single exception of requesting of him that she be allowed to reenlist, she'd been as reclusive as a Ballendian woman was expected to be under such circumstances. It was not, she told herself now, time well spent. She should have spent her time planning what to do when she got back, how to extricate herself from her uncle's guardianship when she did. Even now,

bemoaning the loss of time, she could barely make herself
focus on the future. It was as if her brain froze when she
thought of any future besides the one she'd dreamed of in
the Corps.

Jacinta had stared at the wall vid's order to use the dry
shower and get dressed for a long time before she finally
obeyed. It was, she knew, only the beginning. Even Corps
training conditioned her to obey orders; thinking each order
through was going to be counterinstinctive. But if she didn't
stop complying mindlessly, she'd be swept along by custom. Still, it didn't seem to serve any good purpose to refuse
to get cleaned up and dressed. Finally, she went to the dry
shower, cleansed herself and spent a long time running
her fingers through her hair so that all the strands would
be exposed to the sonics and free of the clinging smoky
smell. Her dirty clothes were gone when she got out, the
lab empty, though someone must have been there to take
her clothes. She picked a pair of rust-colored fatigues from
a stack in a wall bin. They were disposable, but at least they
were soft and clean.

They seemed to have forgotten her. She had sat cross-
legged on the specimen couch for half an hour obeying the
wait here command on the wall vid before jumping down
and padding across the icy floor barefooted to the door.
She was angry with herself. She'd hesitated to get dressed
when ordered to, even though she'd known she couldn't—
wouldn't—step out of the room naked. Then, pleased with
herself for having made the decision herself to get dressed,
she'd sat around forever without even questioning why she
was waiting. This wasn't going to be easy.

In the antechamber, a technician looked up at her from
his workstation. "I thought the event investigator had come
for you," he said. They *had* forgotten her. He touched
his vid, which washed with information Jacinta couldn't
read from across the room. Then the technician shook his
head. "They don't seem to need you anymore. You're
free to go." He ripped a film off the vid and held it out
to her.

She glanced at the patient disposition film just long
enough to see that the only abnormalities noted were a
slight infection in her wrist jacks but that the antibiotic levels were satisfactory for a successful conclusion. "Where's
my duffle?" She was barefooted and had no underwear
under the disposable fatigues.

The technician shrugged.

"I left it in the interrogation room with the event investigator," she explained.

"Then it's still there," he said. He turned back to his vid,
indifferent to her.

Jacinta almost smiled as she turned to walk down the
corridor. The technician obviously didn't realize she was
Lord Santos's niece or even that she was technically a
civilian. The anonymity the Corps had given her had been
a blessing in that she had been treated fairly and without
any deference, which had been a good atmosphere for
learning. She'd had her share of bad times at first because
she simply didn't understand the mechanics and logistics of
being self-sufficient. It had never occurred to her to make
sure she had a clean uniform ready *before* she went to bed
or to buy a vial of her favorite perfumed soap before she ran
out; servants had always laid out her clothes and replaced
soap vials. Before her uncle's servants, when she'd lived
on Ballendo with her parents, there'd been nannies who
worried about the details of living. They'd pick up dirty
clothes, stack films she'd torn from the vid and square the
corners, and pick up dishes and uneaten food and put them
in the recycler. Her homes, the one back at the plantation on
Ballendo and her uncle's, had always been free of dust, but
she hadn't realized that someone must have programmed
the household mechanicals to keep them that way until her
cubey developed a mysterious layer of fine, dry particles
that caused her to fail an inspection. She'd learned then
that there weren't enough mechanicals allotted to ensigns
to clean the cubey frequently enough to pass a particulate
count, but a lint-free mechanic's wipe moistened down with
H_2O and passed over level surfaces did an equally good

job. It hadn't been so difficult to learn to cope with all of this herself, but then, it was either cope or admit defeat by exercising the personal distress clause in her contract with the Corps and return to her uncle's castle. She had been willing to do anything to stay away from the ancestral patriarch, and had succeeded. Until now. Now it was over. There was no more contract with the Corps of Means. The anonymity was fading.

The event interrogation room door wouldn't open for her. Jacinta touched the monitor to ask for entry. "It's Ensign Renya," she said. "May I have my duffle bag?"

The door swung open as the event investigator was getting to his feet. "Lady Jacinta! I didn't realize that was *your* duffle," he said. "It hardly has anything in it. I thought it was Jivar's."

"My hairbrush," Jacinta said, taking the duffle from him, "and shoes. They must have incinerated the clothes we were wearing, they were so filthy." She pulled her spare pair of grip boots out of the duffle and slipped them on her feet.

"Not the clothes *we* were wearing; only the clothes *you* were wearing," Michael said. He was slouched in a straight-backed chair behind the investigator, still wearing muddy grip boots and dirty fatigues. Even his face was smudged with soot from their campfires.

"Stand up, iceman," the investigator growled at him. "This is Lady Jacinta! Surely the Corps taught you to stand in the presence of a Ballendian lady."

Michael stood, his face revealing nothing, but she knew he'd risen only because he'd been ordered. This ability of his to let authority have its way was no small part of his way of surviving in the Corps. Despite his outward passivity, she realized he was very judgmental, quick to think the worst of people. She believed he'd come to like her. She did not want that to change now, not when he was presumably lying through his teeth to this cranky investigator for her benefit. What must he be thinking of her preferential treatment? She'd been given medical attention and allowed to bathe, while, as far as she could tell, he'd sat here with the event investigator, filthy and tired, answering questions that applied equally to her. Now he even had to get to his feet, just because of her.

Jacinta folded the crumpled duffle over her arm and fiddled with the draw tape, wondering what she could say to reassure Michael that wouldn't also be off-putting to the investigator for his having been sensitive to her resuming her civilian status. He, after all, would have no way of knowing that she wasn't happy to be getting out of the Corps. Then she realized, for the first time in three years, that it didn't matter if she offended an officer. With that realization, she knew exactly what to do.

"Investigator," she said, assuming an officerlike tone of voice. "Ensign Jivar is as tired and dirty as I was. Let him bathe and give him fresh clothes before continuing. Surely the Corps wants to treat their own no less well than it treats civilians."

He raised his eyebrows, surprised and perhaps a little perturbed. "Such is a judgment call," the investigator said stiffly. "In my judgment, there is no need. We will be finished with the reports soon enough, then he may take as much time as he likes in the baths."

"Investigator, we both know that the reports will take hours to prepare; there were three officers and a civilian engineer killed, not to mention the two knaves. I was not required to wait until the reports were done to bathe, nor should he be." This wasn't difficult at all. She merely had to say what came to mind. Jacinta smiled slightly at Michael. He was frowning. She glanced back at the Constantinian. He was frowning, too, only very deeply.

"As m'lady is a civilian Ballendian female, Cradle Command contacted your guardian, as is required by Ballendian law," the investigator said. "Your guardian demanded proof of your physical well-being before coming to collect you. Apparently you are, er ... *well*, or I would have been notified to press charges against Ensign Jivar. That is, of course, well and good because now we need only deal with the events related to the two knaves. It is Corps policy to proceed swiftly with such matters, and I trust m'lady understands it is my duty to carry out Corps policy."

"Charges? What kind of charges?" Michael asked.

"I don't recall giving you permission to speak," the investigator said irritably.

"Rape," Jacinta whispered. It hadn't occurred to her that Michael might have been accused if she had not passed the physical examination. "What were your instructions for me if I had not been . . . well?"

"Instructions? Why, nothing unusual, m'lady," the investigator said, smiling maliciously. "Someone from your guardian's household still would have come to collect you, and I would have turned you over to them. Exactly what is occurring, nothing different."

"Except that I'd never be seen or heard from again," she muttered. Jacinta looked at the film that was still in her hand, scanned it again for any unusual comments, frightened now that she had overlooked something.

"That, of course, would be entirely beyond my control," the investigator said. He snapped to attention. "Now if you'll excuse me, in deference to your request, I'll arrange for Ensign Jivar to bathe."

As the investigator stepped over to the console in front of the wall vid, Michael shook his head at Jacinta. "Why did you antagonize him?" he asked, whispering.

"I didn't mean to," she said frantically. "I couldn't just take my duffle bag and say nothing. What would you have thought of me then?"

"I would have thought it was an awkward time to try to talk. Good-bye would have been just fine. As it is, this guy is mad at you and he's going to take it all out on me. So before it gets any worse, you'd better go."

Jacinta glanced at the investigator, who had become involved in a conversation at the console. He was eyeing Jacinta, still frowning.

"Oh, and Jacinta," Michael said, "remember when I said I thought you were stupid for sitting in your cubey alone for three years?"

Jacinta nodded.

"I was wrong. I'm awfully glad you did. I get the feeling it wouldn't have taken much provocation for this Constantinian to fit me for a noose."

"Lady Jacinta, your people are here," the investigator announced suddenly. "They will be in the foyer momentarily." He gestured grandly to the door.

Jacinta looked at Michael. He winked and made a tiny gesture, indicating she should leave.

"I . . ." She bit back more words. Back in the tundra, she'd tried to act like a Ballendian woman. Michael had been confused by her submissiveness, and she'd hated herself for doing it. And just now, she'd deliberately not behaved like a Ballendian woman, and he hadn't liked that either, and it hadn't worked out at all the way she'd hoped it would. Jacinta wet her lips. "Good-bye," she said finally, even though that seemed wholly inadequate for leaving him in a mess. She hoped that the bath the event investigator had begrudgingly consented to would be a tub filled with hot water, not just a dry shower, but that was probably too much to expect.

Jacinta took a slow, deep breath, and walked straight out the door. She had no time even to collect her thoughts before she saw her uncle. A golden light radiated in the featureless foyer, bathing him and his entourage. He was flanked by two Corps guardsmen with green sashes across their chests to indicate their affiliation with the Consortium. Her uncle wore formal Ballendian clothes, heavy cape over a tight-fitting jacket and pants, and kane-hide boots so shiny she could see her own reflection in them. He took one look at her in the papery fatigues, her film in one hand and her duffle in the other, and he shook his head.

"You're not properly dressed!" he said, whipping off his cape. He reached around her to drape it over her shoulders, his fingertips brushing against her chest to pull it straight as he fussily rearranged the folds.

Jacinta felt herself trembling, that nameless horror overtaking her, the one she'd always tried so hard not to think about when it was happening. But no more. She'd learned some things about bad situations in the Corps, and the first lesson was that they didn't go away unless you took action. She grabbed the folds of the cape in her fists, wrenching it out of his fingers. "Don't," she said so sharply that the two guardsmen stirred uneasily.

"Don't cover you? You can't go out onto the tarmac and walk to the windshot wearing a piece of paper," her uncle said.

"You know what I mean don't do," she said, stepping back from him, glaring at him.

The guardsmen shuffled and glanced at each other.

"Are we going to go through this again, Jacinta?" her uncle said. "Your being prissy and rude?"

"I wasn't being rude," she said. "I just don't like anyone to touch me."

"You are being rude," her uncle said. "This very moment. Have you forgotten how to lower your eyes, girl?"

Jacinta was glaring at him. She blinked, realized she actually *had* lost the habit. "In the Corps, I had to look everyone in the eyes, even men."

"Good god, Jacinta, you're home now. Put that military trash behind you. Act like a lady."

"Uncle, maybe this is a mistake. Maybe I should stay in the Corps," she said, hating the whine she felt creeping into her voice. "I have many habits that won't be easily broken, and the jacks . . ."

"You agreed to return peacefully," her uncle said, obviously angry. "I expect that return to mean behaving like a Ballendian lady in every way. And since no Ballendian lady wears jacks, you will, of course, get them removed immediately."

"But I . . ."

He cut her off. "Is it clearly understood? Get the jacks removed. And until they are gone, cover them."

Jacinta sighed. She knew nothing would have changed, least of all her uncle. The sudden foreboding and hopelessness she felt were overwhelming. It had been bad enough when she had first come to Earth to live in her uncle's home and realized she was ill-suited to being a traditional Ballendian lady. She wasn't quite sure why that was so. Her mother had been one, yet Jacinta had not given much thought to tradition when she had lived in her parents' house. Only when her parents died and she'd had to come to Earth had she realized that while Mama had lowered her eyes for Daddy, she, Jacinta, had not been encouraged by her father to do likewise. Certainly she could not understand why her uncle demanded it of her.

Not lowering her eyes had only been the beginning of what seemed like endless clashes. He was nothing like her father, who had trusted her to know that she absolutely must lower her eyes for grandfather Santos but not for grandfather Renya. The differences between her two grand-fathers did not end there. When grandfather Renya held her close, he made her feel warm and safe, just like her father. It had never occurred to her until she had met Uncle Ramon Santos that a man might put his arms around her and make her feel not only unsafe but embarrassed, uncomfortable, and even frightened. She hadn't been quite sure why. Not three years ago when she had left. But now, after having been in the Corps with not much to do but watch holos and read vids, she knew the words that would fit what was happening—and they were ugly, disgusting words. Her father would never have straightened the folds on a cape like her uncle had. Now she knew, and by the look in her uncle's eyes, he knew that she knew.

"You're distraught, which is understandable after your ordeal. Let's get you home," her uncle said. "We can take proper care of you at home."

He reached for her, as if to shepherd her through the foyer, but she walked ahead of him before his fingers could so much as touch her arm. The problem with trying not to comply with every order she was given was that she couldn't do everything at once. She had slipped away from his grasp, but she was walking right into his control. She knew that, but she couldn't think of any alternative. The

Corps would not help her, and the Consortium Authority wouldn't either, probably not even if her uncle were not *the* ultimate Consortium Authority. She was, after all, a Ballendian female—for all practical purposes, a child for the rest of her life.

CHAPTER
4

"The Council of Worlds has gone mad," Lord Ramon Santos muttered as he stared at the decree that was being painted anew on the vid after yet another interruption from the castle activity monitor. He'd read enough of the interrupt to know someone had arrived and was waiting for him, but he didn't give a damn. He was far too concerned about the unexpected decree. "Why didn't you tell me about this the moment it arrived?"

His advisers, all seated around the table, were glancing uneasily at each other. He fixed his eyes on the psyche adviser, Carlos Delgado, who sometimes could be trusted to speak his mind. Not today, apparently. Why was he always surrounded with fools? Didn't they realize that this decree could disrupt Consortium operations for years to come?

"I told them that you ought to be told," Cosimo, his older son, said smugly.

"But you left instructions not to be disturbed," Carlos added hastily. "You said you needed to attend to Lady Jacinta personally, that she was distraught after her ordeal with the knaves. I thought it best to . . ."

"To wait?" Lord Santos said, cutting him off. "How long did you think I would need for my niece? The whole of yesterday and the entire night, too?"

"You didn't specify a time, m'lord," the psyche adviser said lamely, "and you didn't re-emerge."

"That girl can try the patience of a saint," he said, angry even at the memory of trying to talk to her. She had changed a great deal while away, and not for the better. And she'd lost what little sense of fashion and femininity she'd had. Wearing that hideous, brown, sacklike thing when she came to see him. He couldn't imagine where she'd found it, but he'd seen to it she wouldn't find it or anything dowdy in her closets again.

He realized his advisers were still looking at him. He made a dismissing wave of his hand. "She gave me such a headache I went to the baths to relax."

Some chuckled and others nodded as if they understood. They didn't understand, of course. None of them had women in their household as stubborn and foul-tempered as Jacinta. It must be her father's genes, damn royal genes. She surely didn't get it from her mother. Lucinda had always been shy as a rabbit, always freezing up or running away. He had no idea where she'd gotten the courage to elope with Jacinta's father, though it was probably a good thing she had. She'd had Jacinta only thirty weeks later, and they'd been the longest thirty weeks Ramon Santos had ever spent. It had turned out all right, of course. The baby had had the damn royal genes, not his.

"Is someone going to explain how this damned decree happened?" Lord Santos said, drawing himself up in his chair. If he didn't keep them on the subject, they'd happily dither about Jacinta for the next hour.

"It's the local sovereignty issue again," one of the advisers said. It was Grant Litton, the sole Constantinian he kept on his personal board. "The Consortium District is on American soil, and the Americans have a tradition of free elections that dates back to ancient times."

"Yes, but I am the Consortium Leader, and it is I who petitioned Council to seat an ambassador from Earth, not the Americans."

"Of course, they've recognized that in the decree," said the psyche adviser, "by confining the election to the Consortium District. At least they didn't permit all the American states to vote, or even the nations of Earth. Can you imagine the effort a planetwide election would take on Earth?"

Lord Santos grunted. He supposed he ought to be grateful that the Council of Worlds's coffers were not sufficiently filled after the recent Fringe World Wars to consider underwriting planetwide communications on Earth with a net so fine that all the inhabitants could be linked, like they were on most homeworlds. It was ludicrous to think about. Except for a small secessionist territory in the far Southwest, where they actually had some functioning cold-fusion power plants, the rest of the American states were practically Stone Age, and even the Southern Hemisphere nations were nothing more than farmers and hunters. Still, even a small-scale election in just the Consortium District had come as a shock. He had expected simply to appoint himself ambassador and turn leadership of the Consortium over to Cosimo.

"Washington and Brasilia have already sent protests," Cosimo said. "The other nations are sure to do likewise."

"Their protests are meaningless without the Consortium's concurrence," Lord Santos said impatiently. He wondered when his son would appreciate the Consortium's power, and the Council of Worlds's lack of same. He didn't like their focusing on the Earth Consortium so suddenly. They'd certainly been content to leave it in his hands during the war years, happy to collect the taxes from the transport and sale of Earth's antiquities.

"Ensign Michael Jivar is waiting in the anteroom."

It was the soft voice of the brainroom complex, which protocol allowed the activity monitor to use after three visual announcements on the vid failed to bring acknowledgement.

"Who the hell is Ensign Jivar?" Lord Santos demanded,

irritated by the interruption. He wasn't at all certain he liked the new arrangement in the brainroom that had brainjars monitoring doorkeeps. The old human interface would have known better than to disturb a meeting with his advisers.

"The throwback ensign who was with Jacinta when the shuttle crashed," Cosimo replied.

Lord Ramon nodded grimly. He'd almost forgotten that he had yet another unpleasant meeting to face. Damn that girl for putting him in debt to one of those cretins. He'd actually been glad that Jacinta hadn't been harmed, but that had lasted only until he saw her again. Three years of banishment hadn't cured her of wanting to stay in the Corps; even worse, it had changed her from being skittish into being openly defiant. Now he not only had the burden of having her in his household again, but had incurred a blood-debt for the dubious pleasure. At least she had filled out and didn't look like a drowned chicken anymore. If he could keep her out of sackcloth and get her to wear some decent clothes so that men could see her womanly parts, he just might be able to marry her off. He didn't like having rebellious females around. Slow-to-learn sons were bad enough.

"Do you want me to go deal with him, Father?" Cosimo asked him.

"Let him wait," Lord Santos said. "None of us are leaving this room until we figure out how the hell to win an election with Neanderthal voters."

Six of his advisers looked at him blankly, but the seventh, actually an iceman named Morton Green, who had been in Lord Santos's service for many years, nodded and said, "I believe I know a way."

"Let's hear it," Lord Santos said. Sometimes Morton Green provided insights on local matters, though he hated having to look at him. God, he was an ugly brute, with his once-big chest sagging over his breeches like a knocked-up female's.

"You've heard the brainjar's assessment that an election here in the District is most likely to be won by someone who is charismatic . . ."

"Not even my Constantinian competition can claim *that*," Lord Santos said. The rest of the advisers chuckled.

"No, but Master Rayks controls transportation and distribution in the District, and thus controls supplies and goods. We've already seen evidence of his network's increasing frequency of deliveries, which the icers of the Consortium District will welcome. Popularity will do nicely in place of charisma."

"Rayks is a damn thief who has skimmed so much in the past that he has surplus he can use now to make himself look good." Lord Santos pounded his fist on the table, just once, but unable to help that much. He had known for years that Rayks was stealing from the Consortium, but he hadn't seemed to be greedy about it, and he'd provided good transportation for the full musk-oxen hunt, so Lord Santos had never put much effort into exposing him. Now he regretted his decision. He wondered sometimes if Rayks didn't also have some connections with the terrorists. They were known to be almost exclusively icemen, and Rayks had consorted with icers for years.

"Be that as it may," Morton Green said calmly, "he is in a position to gain considerable popularity. You must position yourself likewise to raise your popularity with the icers."

"You're talking about more jobs for the icers," Lord Santos said, shaking his head. "Perhaps by expanding the Chicago excavation?" This was not a new suggestion. Cosimo had suggested it the moment he'd seen the decree, for he'd registered his suggestion with the brainroom.

Cosimo sat up in his chair. "There's a historian from Tosmocal who swears he's located the Art Institute. Our recovery percentage when we sell the artifacts would more than pay the cost."

"I've financed two Art Institute expeditions before," Lord Santos said. "I don't believe it ever existed."

"There is sufficient evidence to believe the Art Institute of Chicago actually existed," the brainroom voice chimed in pleasantly. "Indeed, the very table you are sitting at is known to have been in the Institute's Spanish collection as late as the twenty-second century, a relic from the eighteenth century. It's hand carved from ironwood . . ."

"Stop," Lord Santos said. "Don't you realize that I already know about the furnishings in my own castle? I acquired this table and all the details of its origin ten years ago!"

"No, my Lord, I did not know that. Household records were considered low priority, and have not yet been integrated into the system I represent."

"I may not have been well advised in acquiring your system architecture," Lord Santos said, glaring at Cosimo, who was sitting shame faced across from him. "Confine your discourse to the Tosmocalian's findings and its relationship to the upcoming election."

"The Tosmocalian anthropologist claims to have found evidence that the ill-fated Rejos expedition three years ago was more successful than believed at the time in locating precisely where the ancient building stood. His sinkhole accounted for glacial flow abnormalities beyond what we already have, which, as you pointed out, has already resulted in two expeditions that have failed to uncover any artifacts that can conclusively be traced to the Art Institute building or its contents. However, I have determined that a new expedition would only provide 1,007 new jobs to icemen, including support and incidental work, which is not a sufficient number to sway election results, even if all 1,007 were to vote for Lord Santos. You would need twenty such expeditions to have an even chance against Master Rayks."

The cost of even one more expedition at this time was out of the question. He hadn't sufficient funds, personal or otherwise, something the ambassadorship would have remedied. "Have any other bright ideas?" Lord Santos asked Morton Green.

The big iceman shook his head.

"I have many ideas," the brainroom voice said.

Brainrooms always did. Too many. Lord Santos sighed. "Break them down into five categories, and give us the top five in each, along with the pros and cons."

"The five categories are . . ."

"Not verbally. Give us a display."

The vid flushed and began painting lists in a size that would be easy to read even from the far end of the ironwood table, for the vid could use the entire east wall for its displays, as it did now. The holo views of a Ballendian playground disappeared, and were replaced with lists that could easily be scanned.

"You're being far too general," Lord Santos complained as he read. "What do you mean there under the personal popularity caption by *increased affiliation* with the icemen?"

"May I speak?"

"Of course you may speak," Lord Santos said. "I just asked you to, didn't I?"

"I'm directed to address the irritation in your voice by reminding you that, having this interchange as reference, I'm not likely to have doubts about your instructions in the future, unless, of course, you are not consistent in your behavior. The brainroom masters beg your indulgence while I am still learning."

"Go on," Lord Santos said tiredly.

"There are a number of ways to increase your personal affiliation with icers. On a small scale, but one which I calculate would have some effect, would be to learn the names of servants in the castle and to greet them by name. You could even inquire about their chores and compliment them on their efficiency, though I'd recommend doing the latter only if you sincerely feel the work is being done well. Having kitchen staff members purchase local produce as much as possible, and inviting icer merchants to compete with offworld imports are other possible opportunities. Family members who have secret liaisons with icer females might become more public about them."

"What secret liaisons?" Lord Santos said, sitting bolt upright in his chair.

"What about this other category of increasing the icers' standard of living?" Cosimo said quickly.

"What secret liaisons?" Lord Santos repeated, silencing his son with a look.

"Protocol forbids elaboration on specific incidents, but in general, if you or your family members were romantically involved with icers, especially if such involvement were to lead to marriage before the election . . ."

"Marriage!" Lord Santos said, shocked.

"Yes, marriage," the brainroom voice confirmed. "Your acceptance of such a union is calculated to raise your popularity with seventy-one point five percent of all voting icers. Icemen are family oriented. Your status as a widower rings a certain sympathetic chord in their culture, which can be exploited by your taking a bride from their ranks. You have two unmarried sons whose marriages to icer women could bring similar results. I realize that in Ballendian culture Anselem is not of marriageable age, but in the icers' culture, even a boy of thirteen marries. Cosimo is considered marriageable in both cultures, as are you."

"What about these secret liaisons you alluded to? How do those contribute to my election campaign?"

"They do not contribute at all if they are kept secret. You should be aware, however, that they represent great risk if exposed as nothing more than sexual trysts."

"What's the risk of exposure?" Lord Santos asked, completely convinced at this point that Cosimo was involved in such an affair. The boy couldn't even lift his eyes. At least he had the decency to feel shame.

"Icers living in the District are required to submit their infants to genecoding within two weeks of birth, and such coding, of course, identifies both parents, and thus exposure of the starborn father. Empirical data shows that very few such unions have ever officially resulted in offspring, even though there are no biological reasons why icer women, who are known to have high fertility rates and to consort with starborn men, do not register their children. The matter is currently under investigation, but . . ."

"Am I at risk?" Lord Santos asked, cutting off the voice. This brainjar had not been equipped with local variances, or it would have known that the investigation was merely a procedural cover; every starborn man in Cradle City knew why those women didn't register the bastards.

"I do not have sufficient data to know," the brainroom voice said.

"I wasn't asking you," Lord Santos said.

Cosimo shook his head without even looking up.

"Enough said," Lord Santos said. He made a dismissive gesture. "Now what of these other lists?"

They continued for another hour, discussing the lists and selecting action plans with the best odds for success. Lord Santos concluded the meeting when the brainroom voice told them that all the plans put together resulted in slightly less than fifty-fifty odds for his winning the election. It wasn't good enough, but he didn't have the resources to compete with Rayks's network, and he had no intention of marrying an icewoman to take advantage of the only plan that offered better odds. Too drained to continue, Lord Santos dismissed his advisers. When Cosimo got up with them, he waved him back into his chair.

"You can just imagine what I want to talk to you about," Lord Santos said when the portal sealed behind the last adviser.

"Yes, sir," Cosimo said from abject posture.

"There are perfectly good brothels in Cradle City with starborn companions who are physically incapable of bearing offspring. Why would you want to do it with one of those gargantuan female natives who have fertility rates like rabbits?"

"They aren't gargantuan where it makes a difference in sex," Cosimo said defensively.

"Don't give me any smart-ass remarks, boy. This is a serious matter. Cradle City's inhabitants will be voting in this election, too, and though there are less starborn in the District than icers, their number is not insignificant. They would not think well of me for letting you mix starborn genes with Neanderthal genes."

"I make sure they don't get pregnant," Cosimo said amiably.

"They?" Lord Santos stared at his son. "More than one?"

"Not at the same time," Cosimo said.

"Until this election is over, I insist you take no chances. Get rid of this girl—or girls."

"Are you going to stop seeing your Constantinian mistress?"

"What?"

"Farley Degeen, your Constantinian administrator at the Consortium. She is your mistress, isn't she?"

"Of course not. My relations with Farley are strictly business."

"A female administrator?" Cosimo said.

Lord Santos shrugged. "You will learn as time goes on that we cannot always choose our associates in interplanetary commerce. Farley is not my idea of a good mistress; I doubt that any non-Ballendian woman could be. And while I would not have chosen women for any posts in the Consortium's administration, I did inherit a few who have proven valuable. Farley is one of them. And if I did have a Constantinian mistress, she wouldn't also be a business associate who would be in a position to do irreparable damage to me."

"What is a maid going to do to damage me, or even you?"

"Spit in your morning cup, maybe put used feathers in your bed. Who knows? What's worse right now is that she'll speak ill of you in the City Under, and that will reflect poorly on me. Pay her off generously, Cosimo, and be done with her."

Cosimo sighed and nodded. "Yes, sir," he said as he pushed the chair back from the ironwood table.

"And send the cretin in to me on your way out," Lord Santos added. He stayed seated at the head of the table, waiting for the iceman turned Corps of Means ensign, thinking more about the dilemma of not being able to increase his chances for success in the election than what he might have to pay this iceman for saving Jacinta's life.

At least he didn't lumber through the portal. He wasn't much over six feet tall, but he stood straight, with his shoulders thrown back, so he still had that unmistakable iceman size, though he carried it more gracefully than most. With his cap tucked under his left arm, his hair trimmed neatly in military style, one might almost think he was a starborn whose size was inseparably related to some other desirable trait, which usually set one to wondering what that trait might be. The iceman stuck out his hand in Ballendian greeting, so Lord Santos assumed he'd been briefed in Ballendian customs. He shook hands with him, noting the firm grip. Pushy lunk.

"I hope you'll excuse my tardiness. I wouldn't have kept you waiting but for matters of grave importance," Lord Santos said, certain the iceman could not be adept in detecting lies. That was a starborn cultivation, which only a small segment of the population claimed. He believed there was little risk in heeding the brainroom's suggestion to increase his affiliations with the icers. Might as well start now, even if it was with an apology that was a lie.

"Of course," Ensign Jivar said, amiably enough, but unable to hide his surprise.

Careful now. He wished he'd taken the time to learn this boy's intelligence quotient. How much brains did it take to recognize patronizing?

"Sit down," Lord Santos said, gesturing to the chair on his left. The ensign sat, putting his cap on his lap, his body held rigid. His muscles were taut and strong, the usual icer gauntness gone after some years in the Corps of Means. His face was pleasant if not handsome; only a slightly Roman nose gave character to his dark-haired icer appearance that even the Corps uniform and training did not hide. "You saved my niece's life, and I am in your debt. Such service must be rewarded."

"I ask no reward for doing my duty, sire," the ensign said.

Lord Santos raised his brows. "Duty? Since when does an iceman consider risking his life for a starborn woman as his duty?"

"The Lady Jacinta is a Corps navigator. Any Corpsman knows navigator talent and training is valuable and must be preserved," he replied. "Such inherent qualities are, as you know, quite rare. It was my duty to save her."

Lord Santos stared at Ensign Jivar. It was not the expected answer from an iceman. Had Corps training really reached past this youth's icer background? Lord Santos assumed that he was unusual for an iceman. He'd have to be even to have become a mere firefighter in the Corps. "How did you manage to be accepted in the Corps of Means? I didn't even know they considered applications from . . . Earthlings."

"It's my understanding that they do not encourage such applications and do not solicit them, but if they are properly sponsored by a starborn, they do consider them. Such was my case," he said, rubbing his hand against his breeches, as if he knew that the icer herald was completely inadequate. "Lord Rejos of Ballendo sponsored me."

"Now I know who you are," Lord Santos said. "That iceman's son. The one who stayed behind when all the others had fled, just because he had that brainjar in his clothes. I had almost forgotten about that incident." Not really, but he *had* tried to forget. Rejos had been the scion of a fine Ballendian family, but he'd been involved in blatantly criminal activities. But for the distance to Ballendo and his family's reputation, he might have been jailed instead of merely fined. It had annoyed Lord Santos greatly that Rejos had not seemed to appreciate the leniency with which he'd been dealt. There had been some poetic justice in his dying during one of his looting expeditions, but the satisfaction Lord Santos had felt ended when they found the brainjar on the iceman. It was a personal affront to realize the ungrateful wretch had deliberately squandered his sponsorship on an iceman instead of using it for Jacinta, as he had promised.

"Yes, my father died with Lord Rejos," the ensign said.

"Not exactly with him, as I recall," Lord Santos said. "Rejos was below, trapped by the glacier flow when the lift shaft failed. Your father was above."

"That is so," the ensign said. "He waited for help."

"So the story goes," Lord Santos said, not even trying to hide the scoff in his voice. "But personally I've always believed he waited for Rejos to die. If the intent had been for Rejos to live, he would have turned on the transponder, and help would have come in time."

"But there was no transponder," the ensign said, ruffled at last.

"Rejos would have had to have been stupid to go out on the ice sheet without a transponder. He was a fool, but he was not stupid."

"If there had been a transponder, my father would be alive," the ensign insisted.

"Oh, yes, and since he was such an honorable fellow, it would have been him standing here now, instead of you."

"I should think you would hope so," the ensign said, his composure regained. "It was my father who first taught me the meaning of honor and duty, even Ballendian honor."

Lord Santos looked hard at the icer turned ensign, but saw no malice in his face. He let the rebuke go in favor of pondering what to do next.

So why was this iceman who knew the worth of a blood-debt not invoking a new one eagerly? If he had any intelligence at all, he had to know he wouldn't go far in the Corps without a living sponsor. Asking Santos to replace Rejos was an obvious demand. Maybe he had overestimated the boy's understanding of what he was offering. "I am, despite your protest of duty, grateful that the Lady Jacinta has returned safely to Castle Santos. I am in your debt."

"I'm just glad I was in a position to assure the Lady Jacinta's safe return," the ensign said blandly.

"Surely there is something I can do to express my appreciation," Lord Santos said, not accepting even for a moment that the ensign's sense of duty was genuine or the debt truly unrecognized. Not by an iceman who wore a Corps uniform because of a blood-debt.

"Nothing, sire. The Corps supplies all that I required. I have a brief furlough, and then I'll return to *Ship Lisbon.* I have everything I need."

"A place to stay?" Lord Santos suggested, irritated now because the boy seemed determined not to accept payment of the blood-debt. He didn't like leaving those open with strangers. You never knew when they'd call it in, nor how.

"I thought to stay at the hostel in Cradle," the ensign said.

"Corps or no, you'd be turned away because of your icer herald," Lord Santos said brusquely.

"I had not considered that," the ensign said thoughtfully.

"Stay here in the castle," Lord Santos said. "Perhaps we'll have an opportunity to speak again." He couldn't, after all, offer to pay a debt until it was recognized.

"I would be honored to accept your hospitality," the ensign said. "Thank you."

"Brainroom, send someone who can guide Ensign Jivar to a guest suite," he said. And to the ensign, "We'll expect you at dinner tonight in the family dining room."

"Thank you, sire. That would be very nice. Will the Lady Jacinta be there, too?"

Lord Santos frowned, not pleased to hear an iceman inquiring about his niece. Still, the brainroom's strategy included many distasteful plans. "Yes, Jacinta will be there," he said.

The servant entered the meeting room and waited silently. When Lord Santos noticed him with a glance, the liveried iceman's head bowed politely.

"Take Ensign Jivar to the blue guest room in the family wing," Lord Santos said.

The servant chanced a curious glance at the ensign's wrist, and his eyebrows raised perceptibly when he saw the icer herald. "As you wish, sire."

The contempt in the man's voice was no doubt meant for the ensign, something to do with below-stairs snobbery, which Lord Santos knew existed but didn't pretend to understand. "You're . . . John Winter, aren't you?"

Surprised to be addressed by name, the servant nodded. He couldn't see the screen behind him with his name painted there then quickly erased by the brainroom.

"Make certain my staff understands that Ensign Jivar is to be treated with the honor due a man who has saved the life of Lady Jacinta."

"Of course, sire," the servant said, bowing deeply from the waist. Then he turned to the ensign. "If you'll follow me, sir?"

The ensign rose, bowed slightly to Lord Santos. Lord Santos smiled and nodded to signify final dismissal. He watched the two icemen depart, one in his own gray and scarlet livery, the other in the rust and gray of the Corps. The servant slunk in the characteristic icer gait. But not Jivar. He was a cool one. In surroundings that should cower all icemen and even a lowly ensign of any origin, Jivar walked after the lackey with confidence.

"You've been listening, brainroom?" he asked when the portal sealed.

"Of course."

"How would the elections be affected by a marriage between my niece and that iceman?"

"Which iceman? There were two present."

"The Corpsman, of course."

"Your niece is not as well known in City Under as you or your sons, but Ensign Michael Jivar is almost legend as the first iceman to be accepted into the Corps. His name is known to all of them. Despite Lady Jacinta's anonymity, I calculated a seventy-seven percent favorable vote."

"Seventy-seven percent?" Lord Santos could not help but be amazed. That would cinch the election. "She's a headstrong girl. I don't think I could force her into such a union."

"But there are steps to be taken to encourage her."

"Such as?"

"Given their recent adventure together, the lady is bound to be feeling some gratitude herself toward the young man. They spent nearly forty consecutive hours together after the deaths of their companions and thus are not likely to be strangers to one another anymore."

"He didn't touch her," Lord Santos said stiffly. "Physical examinations proved that."

"Love is preceded by getting acquainted. I merely meant that we have a base from which to work. They are already acquainted, and may have even grown to like one another, however slightly. Given Lady Jacinta's rebellious nature, I calculate a fifty-fifty chance of her falling in love with the iceman, partly in defiance of you, for she would believe such behavior would displease you. I'd caution you not to disillusion her too quickly. To increase the odds slightly, put him in the guest suite next to the Lady Jacinta's suite so that they will share a balcony. This will give them more opportunities to be alone together."

"Intercept that . . . whatever his name was, and have him take the ensign to the red room."

"John Winter."

"What?"

"The servant's name was John Winter."

"Yes. Him. Do it!"

"It's done."

CHAPTER
5

The servant left Michael in a room so splendid Michael could only stand with his cap in his hands and stare. He should have known better than to think he'd gleaned all there was to know about the starborn's penchant for comfort and aesthetics by sneaking into the officers' lounge on *Ship Lisbon*; there was, after all, a civilian hierarchy with which he had little experience. If he had thought about it, he wouldn't have surmised anything like this. It wasn't just the gold-and-red-lacquered walls that seemed to disappear into vaulted shadows; he could not see seams at the doorway or quite make out the outline of recesses from which light flooded the room. The furnishings were few and unfamiliar, though he guessed their purposes. He wasn't at all sure he could sleep soundly on something that looked more like a corral of golden feathers than a bed, but he sat down in one of the big gilded chairs and leaned back against what he believed to be natural red fur. No Terran animal had a pelt like this; the cost of transporting a chair like this through the starlanes must have been staggering. It gave him excellent support, its seat and back motile, shaping itself to fit the small of his back and the hollow between his shoulders. No doubt somewhere in the chair was a brainjar calibrating the pressure to take his body weight into account, for he actually felt the seat lifting him a bit higher, perhaps to account for his height. For a moment he wasn't sure what to do with his cap; it didn't seem to belong in his hands while he was luxuriating in the chair, so he flicked it onto the golden bed. He instantly regretted this action. The feathers undulated around the cap, feathery fingers tugging at the brim as if to drag it down into the depths. Alarmed, Michael got up from the chair to snatch the cap out of the bed before it disappeared beneath the feathers. Golden feathers now dived to fill in the place where the cap had been, and in just a few seconds no trace of the disturbance remained.

Michael placed the cap carefully on the seat of the chair he had just vacated, and watched it for a moment to be sure it was safe. The chair didn't do anything to the cap; it must be too light to activate the brainjar. Satisfied, he stepped over to the red metal drapes. They were secondary artillery shields, and he knew where to find the pressure-sensitive seams that would stimulate the brain-controlling operating mechanism. They folded at his touch. Behind the drapes was a glass wall with a metallic shimmer separating his room from a garden-filled balcony, a very large balcony onto which he realized opened at least one other suite of rooms.

Michael took a deep breath, stepped through the passglass, and smiled. Before the Academy, he had not known he could step through; he had thought that the ability to do so was starborn magic to which he would never be privy. He still did not understand this particular technology, but he now knew that passglass was not magic.

Standing on the balcony he could smell the scent of the pine forest being wafted up from below, the scent of home, mingling with flowery perfumes from a perfusion of red blossoms he did not recognize. Off-world imports, perhaps Ballendian. He knew incoming cargo ships never deadheaded to Earth, despite the outrageous costs of their cargoes. They never deadheaded outbound either, though legally there was nothing but the minor curiosity of quivat to export. Under the guise of saving antiquities, the Consortium managed to export quite a lot.

He walked to the polished granite rail; the ground sloped away just under the balcony, too far to jump safely, too far even to hear any noise from City Under. To the east, a few open campfires already sparkled in the shadowy place at the edge of the pine forest, where spiky pine and fir gave way to the thick crosshatch pattern of hedgerows. He could see the glint of the fires reflecting from greenhouse glass, too. And in the north was a black band of trees contrasting with the seemingly endless expanse of the glaciers. They glittered, crags and spires of ice catching the last light of day like gems, tantalizingly beautiful.

"Michael!"

It was Jacinta calling to him, and Michael turned. Had she not spoken first, he would not have recognized the starborn lady standing by the passglass panels. She wore a fine, green sari draped gracefully over her body, held in place at the shoulder with jade. Her eyes were green, a shimmering, unnatural green, even where the whites should be. The stare of starborn women gave most icers chills, for most did not realize it was through lenses that they used as adornment. The Corps had shattered Michael's superstitions, but his instinct to distrust the starborn had never fully left him. "M'lady," he said cautiously. He had not expected to see her before dinner, and certainly not on his balcony.

"Well, I see that it worked. He invited you to stay. But how . . . interesting to find you sharing my balcony," she said, not sounding pleased.

"You mean my being an iceman? A Neanderthal?" It was reflexive in him, the anger always lurking just beneath the surface, especially coming so close on the heels of his interview with her uncle, and that fresh from the Constantinian's investigation. He just couldn't help it.

"Michael, don't be an ass," she snapped. "It's your gender I'm worried about, not your origins. Sharing a balcony where we could go into each other's rooms without being observed is a circumstance my uncle would not normally permit."

Michael didn't like being called an ass, either, but somehow it didn't sting so much.

"Perhaps a mistake . . . ?"

"Hardly," she said with a rueful laugh. "One of us is being set up. It's just hard to tell if it's you, so that he'd not lose face by sending you packing because you insulted his honor, or if it's me, so that he'll have an excuse to punish me."

"Wouldn't he have to see me . . . us do something dishonorable? We seem to be alone."

"There are many eyes and ears in my uncle's castle, not all of them human. Never assume you're alone."

"Then he could be listening to this conversation?"

"He could be. Or to be more precise, he might think he is. I deafened my suite, which included the balcony," she said, smiling mischievously. "Navigator jacks work perfectly well on brainjars in civilian brainrooms, too."

"What happens if he finds out?"

Even in the twilight he could see that she paled. But then she squared her shoulders. "I'm good at what I do," she said. "I left no traces in the brainjars."

"If you're so good," he said, "it shouldn't be too difficult to find out which one of us he's trying to trap, and how. For example, is my suite bugged, too? Are there any unusual alarm logs established for either of us?"

"Why does a firefighter know so much about brainroom monitoring?" she said so quickly that he didn't think she wanted to consider his suggestion.

"How did you think fires were reported to us?"

"Oh," she said, "through the monitors, of course." She nodded and shrugged. "Stay here, Michael. Look at the scenery or something until I get back. I did it once; I can do it again." She smiled, but it wasn't really a reassuring one. She seemed jittery.

It took her a long time, at least it seemed a long time to Michael. As daylight waned, lights on the glacier waxed, melt stations and mining camps, always so pretty from afar but chilling to the soul. In rare warm years, his family had scavenged along the terminus for metal the river of ice brought down from ancient cities in the north, but stickmen patrolled the perimeters now. The milky ice sheet and all its contents were being protected from looters, they said. Yet when *they* carried anything away, they didn't call it looting. They called it taking the necessary action to preserve artifacts for all humankind. He'd seen one of the museums on Whitney Planet; he hadn't seen any of the metal rods he'd watched his father break loose from frozen cement casements, just shards of pottery and shelves of plastic. The museums, he knew, were getting only what the Consortium couldn't sell to private collectors, of which, it seemed, the Treaty Worlds were full.

"I think you'd better leave."

Jacinta's voice barely penetrated his reverie.

"What?"

"Leave," she said. She was standing before the passglass, looking pale in the artificial light, angry. "Leave now, tonight."

Michael felt a sinking feeling beneath his solar plexus. She had that same resolute expression that she'd worn for hours after the murders on the tundra. "What's wrong?"

She looked at him blankly.

"That look on your face . . . I figured he plans to end the blood-debt by killing me. Does it involve you, too?"

"Yes, I mean, no. He's not going to kill either of us."

"Then what . . . ?"

Jacinta couldn't look at him. She shook her head, but then ended up blurting it out anyway. "He's going to use me—us—to win the elections!"

"The ambassadorial election?" And when she nodded, he said, "How?"

"Never mind. It's too embarrassing. I can't believe even he would stoop this low," she said. She put her hands over her face, obviously distressed. In a moment she got hold of herself, and her fingers pressed together in an almost prayerlike gesture. "You've got to leave."

"How are you going to help him win the election?" Michael said. "How am *I* going to help him? I'm an iceman, nothing, nobody."

"I know," she said. "Oh, damn, that's not what I mean. Look, he's not just keeping you around because of the blood-debt. It's the election."

Michael allowed himself a slight smile. "I'm aware that having an iceman as a guest could endear your uncle to certain factions in the Consortium, and perhaps even to icers." He shrugged. "I can't help that, and neither can you. But don't worry. It's not going to win the election for him."

She was breathing deeply, still agitated. "It will take more than patronizing to get him by this time. But then, you haven't been down to City Under since we got back. You probably don't know what's going on."

"Probably not. The inquests and the reports took every moment since I got back; for some reason I had to do them alone," he said, still amazed that even Lord Santos had had the power to extricate his niece from Corps routines. "When I did get finished, Lord Santos's summons was waiting." He opened his palms in a gesture. "Here I am. Mystified! Whatever did you find out when you plugged in."

"He's determined to be the only authorized representative for Earth in the Council of Worlds as well, for which he needs the Earth ambassador seat. Of course, the Council is sending an election team. His advisers tell him he doesn't have a chance to win unless he also wins some popularity with the icers, because it's going to be a free election for the entire District."

Michael reflected a moment. "I don't think I'll be that much help to him," he said politely. Even though isolated incidences of kindness to icers were rare and interesting news among icers, the suspicions and distrust were not easily unseated.

"Not alone, you can't. But, just as I bought him his seat as the head of the Consortium, he plans for me to buy his seat in Council as Earth's ambassador."

"I don't see . . ."

Jacinta cut him off. "As one of three candidates for the head of the Consortium when the war against the Fringe Worlds started, my uncle had gained tremendous popularity by insisting that I, his niece, the fair Lady Jacinta, whose genetic traits gave me the gift of stellar navigation, be inducted into the Corps for wartime training. The announcement was very well received by the Consortium, and even the Council of Worlds. I was indeed inducted and trained, but you know I never saw combat. I occasionally navigated in the trade lanes, usually when *Ship Lisbon* was carrying nothing more important than supplies for Ballendians living on outpost worlds like Earth. More frequently I co-piloted shuttles, raising cargo to *Ship Lisbon* or hauling passengers planetside. My life was never in the slightest danger. Even so, it's my uncle who got the recognition for making a sacrifice. It would seem that I'm about to be offered up again. The only way to stop it is for you to leave. I *won't* be used by him again, not like this."

"Like how?" Michael asked. "I can understand that letting you be inducted into the Corps would work to his benefit, and we'll put aside for the moment that it also worked to yours, because getting into the Corps was your goal, too. Obviously, whatever he has planned this time doesn't please you so much, so tell me, how will my lady serve her uncle this time?" When she frowned so intensely, he wondered if it had been a mistake for him to presume on the camaraderie they'd known in the tundra.

"By marrying an iceman," she said. She looked up at him. "You. Can you believe that?"

Michael flinched. Trying not to look unnerved, he said, "That would raise Lord Santos's popularity in City Under. But wouldn't he be the object of ridicule in Cradle and even back on Ballendo?"

"Once he's ambassador, who would dare?" she said. "There isn't any higher seat of power. The gall of that man. I cannot believe that even he would stoop so low."

Michael tried to control his anger. He hated her cavalier

dismissal of marrying him, but Lord Santos's manipula-
tions of the icers' goodwill infuriated him. Such a marriage
would be received by icers as a statement of acceptance, and
having no true candidate of their own, he knew they would
vote for Lord Santos. That was unthinkable to Michael;
having any starborn representing Earth in the Council of
Worlds was unthinkable, and already he was seeing a way
to prevent it. He looked at Jacinta. She was as angry as he
was, but for far different reasons. He didn't blame her for
not wanting to be manipulated and used by her uncle, and
he sympathized with her because her circumstances were
unique even among the starfarers. Just by accident of being
born a Ballendian woman, she had less right to control her
own destiny than he did even as an icer. Until meeting
her, he'd never given a thought to Ballendian women's
plight; indeed, even now, he didn't know if other Ballendian
women felt constrained by the bloodlaws, for Jacinta was
the only Ballendian woman he knew. He shouldn't care,
but he did.

"Jacinta," he said slowly. "Don't be so quick to dismiss
your uncle's plan. It could get you back into the Corps."

"What?" She looked at him, aghast or amazed? He wasn't
sure with those lenses hiding her pupils.

"Are you sure we can't be heard?" he asked.

"Positive," she said. "Your suite is safe now, too. I
deafened the ears. They can see us though, so be careful
how you act."

What's that supposed to mean? he almost asked, but he
didn't. He crossed his arms over his chest. "Doesn't he have
to turn over your pedigree or whatever they call it to your
husband when you marry?"

"Papers," she said. "They're purely ceremonial. What
gets turned over is me, and that's Ballendian law."

"I'm in the Corps," he said simply. "Why are you hesi-
tating?"

He heard her suck in her breath, perhaps in shock, but
she seemed to be considering, her head cocked, her brow
furrowed. He was in the Corps, which is where she wanted

to be. As his wife, she could be, too. The Corps was, in fact, predisposed to encourage family bonding within the ranks. "Why would you do this?" she asked. "I know icers don't like my uncle or any starfarer for that matter. Wouldn't you be betraying your people?"

"The alternative is Master Rayks. He's worse than your uncle."

"My uncle is the lesser of two evils?"

Michael nodded.

"But if neither of them got enough votes, the Council of Worlds would say Earth isn't ready for a seat, and things would go on as they are."

"Rayks would get enough votes," Michael said. "He controls most of the employment, which icers need to survive. They can neither grow enough crops to support themselves nor trade outside the District without transportation, which Rayks also controls. He even controls the city under Cradle, the rents, the rights to pitch a tent."

"But even if it's not bad for your people, or not as bad as Rayks might be, isn't it wrong to manipulate them?"

Michael squirmed. Of course it was, but he couldn't tell her that. He shrugged.

"There must be something in it for you," she said suspiciously.

"Your hand," he said with a smile, charmingly.

"That's what I thought," she said, shaking her head.

"What you're thinking is not what I meant," he said, disgusted. "This marriage would have to appear to be genuine or it would be useless for your uncle's purposes. He has to want to win this election quite a lot to throw a blood relative away on a Neanderthal. I was speaking to his fantasy, not any of mine."

"At least you haven't any illusions about what he really thinks of you."

"And quickly getting over any I may have had about what you think of me," he said bitterly.

"Oh, there you go again. Look at it from my viewpoint. What good is it going to do me to simply exchange one male master for another? And even if I did, you've been in the Corps long enough to know that a navigator married to a kettle tender wouldn't advance in rank very much, if at all. It wouldn't reflect well on you either."

It was true. There was a very real class system in the Corps, even if the regulations stated otherwise. "The problem can be solved by my not invoking the right to bond. You'd be a free agent."

She picked a decorative rock out of the flower pot at her elbow and turned it over in her hand, worrying it. "Even if I trusted you to do that, my first question still stands. What's in it for you?"

He hesitated. "I need a sponsor," he finally said.

"You'd never have gotten in if you didn't have a sponsor," she said.

"He's dead. I get to stay, but I'll never attain any rank to speak of without an active sponsor. Marrying you would give me your uncle at the least, maybe others."

Jacinta seemed relieved. "You'd get sponsors all right, and I could stay in the Corps. But how do I know I can trust you?"

"To not invoke the bond?"

She nodded. "Nor to take any . . . advantage of the situation."

"Dammit, if I had wanted to take advantage of you, I had my chance out on the tundra, didn't I?"

"Not really. You knew we'd be rescued, and that there'd be an inquest."

"Jacinta, I was the only one at the inquest, and I lied for you. What have I ever done to make you think I would hurt you in any way?"

"You lied for me," she said. "What else might you do?"

"You lied, too," he said, furious with her now. "And how do I know you're not lying about how much your uncle wants this marriage? What if I go to ask for your hand, and he has me shot for offending his precious honor? You are, after all, a Ballendian lady, and I'm a Neanderthal."

For a moment she was silent. "I'm sorry," she said

finally. "You warned me not to treat you like a Ballendian man, and I just did, and you misunderstood. A Ballendian man would have offered his oath, and that would be all that I'd need to go ahead."

"I'm not a goddamned Ballendian. I'm a Neanderthal. We aren't supposed to have any honor," he said.

"I already know better," she said. "You lied for me."

"A minute ago I could have sworn you were holding that against me," he said.

"No," she said. "It's even written in the bloodlaws that a man may use any means to uphold a woman's honor. A Ballendian would have understood; I'm sorry you didn't. Just give me your word that you'll not invoke the right to bond; that's all I need."

"You have it," he said.

"Then as long as that's settled, let me put your fears to rest about my uncle possibly not being pleased. First, remember that I'm damn good at sneaking around in the brainjars. I had years alone in my cubey to figure out how it could be done, so by the time I got my jacks, it was easy for me. My uncle has less than a one percent chance of discovering that I know his plan. The plan is a good one, and I promise you that he will be ecstatic when you ask him for my hand. He has the finest psychological constructs I've ever seen in his brainjars, and they've told him that I have a fifty percent chance of falling in love with a likable ensign, who also happened to have saved my life."

"If those were odds on a shuttle safely de-orbiting and reaching the ground, I'd not get on," Michael said.

"Neither would I, but obviously we have complete control. Given my falling in love, there's almost an eighty percent chance of my considering marriage, possibly out of gratitude, perhaps even in defiance of custom."

"I think the eighty percent is too low, given defiance of custom. Bet they'd raise the odds if they'd seen you on the tundra."

Jacinta lowered her eyes, blushing.

"You may not want to be a Ballendian woman," Michael

said softly, "but you are, aren't you."

"Not for long," she said hopefully, yet somehow fiercely. "I've had years to study, but no chances to practice being anything else. I can be done with dreaming about it and really start doing it, if this works."

"If? Look, the first thing you have to do is convince yourself that it will work. If you have doubts, obstacles look insurmountable, and the next thing you know, they really are."

"Oh, yes, mindset," she said impatiently. "I've learned about that, too." She turned her wrists to look at her jacks, which had a magnificent filigree of lacy wires covering the heads.

"I didn't know it had a name," he said. "Mindset. That fits, all right, but knowing its name isn't the same as having it. Just remember that if you falter in it, it's my life at risk, not yours. Having a couple of Ballendian sponsors isn't worth risking my life, at least not to me."

"There'll be a dowry," she said, suddenly sounding desperate. "You can have it."

Michael shook his head. "That's bribery."

"I won't falter," she said emphatically.

Michael smiled. "That's mindset." At least, he hoped it was. "So forget about the dowry. The hand of the fair Lady Jacinta is prize enough."

She didn't look happy.

"What's the matter? You're getting into the Corps. Isn't that what you wanted?"

"Look, Michael, you said it yourself, that I am a Ballendian woman, whether I like it or not. I know this marriage has to appear as if we are in love, that it's genuine. But don't think that I would ever . . ."

"Ever what?" he asked angrily, though he knew perfectly well what she meant.

The lenses glittered, but she remained poised, silent.

"My herald may be unclassified in your geneticists' records, but it makes me no less a man than any starborn. I respond favorably to an attractive woman, but it doesn't follow that I'm some kind of savage who would want any but a woman who was willing, even one who called herself my wife. I'll excuse you this time for thinking that I might." He calmed himself. "I think we're even on that score."

Jacinta flushed and lifted the shawl of her sari to her head. "I don't know what kind of person a native Earthling might be; I don't pretend to know anything about your people. But I believe I can trust a Corpsman to keep his word."

"Even a kettle tender?" he said.

"Especially a kettle tender," she said.

"Then you have my word as Ensign Jivar that I won't force you into my bed. But this deal is off if you won't leave me my pride and grant that it's possible you may come willingly."

He heard her suck in her breath and thought she'd probably cut off an angry reply. He thought for a moment he had pushed her too far; her knuckles were white around the rock. But finally, she said, "It's settled, then." She cleared her throat and looked at him. "How shall you court me, Ensign Jivar?"

The bargain was costing her much in pride, Michael thought sadly. That she was willing to pay indicated how badly she wanted her career in the Corps. That wasn't supposed to matter to him, since it had turned out well for him, but somehow it did.

"I never court ladies who keep rocks in their hands; never know when they might have a mind to bash my head in with it."

She let the rock fall from her hand; it clattered off the balcony and down the slope. It wasn't a rock at all; it was a bit of marble, perfectly spherical, the kind his father had brought him from a melt when he was a child. He picked another from the flowerpot and handled it to her. She looked at him, probably puzzled, though the damnable lenses hid so much expression.

"I'd say we have begun admirably, m'lady. Who could know what pleasant conversation may have taken place here on our balcony?" He picked up another marble, and threw it out over the edge of the city. It dropped out of sight and clattered below. "Any watcher could only speculate on what has led up to the ensign giving the Lady Jacinta a marble to throw over the balcony. It's innocent enough and just a trifle beyond the formality that would have prevailed had you been unreceptive to my presence on your balcony."

Jacinta tossed the marble, accepting another that Michael handed her. "You'll be dining with the family tonight. My uncle can be trusted to behave cordially, since his advisers have explained to him that any hint of disapproval could frighten you off. But I don't know if my cousins know of my uncle's plans, so they . . . well, just sit next to me if you can."

"Of course. Where else would an infatuated man sit?"

"At my uncle's table, wherever he's told to sit," she said.

She picked up a handful of marbles, throwing spheres of antiquity in rapid succession.

Michael felt guilty for having started this game, but he didn't have the heart to stop her. She picked up more and Michael watched her throw.

"After dinner, we could retire to my chambers for a game of chess. My uncle's spies will surely take note."

"Isn't that a bit risky? I don't pretend to understand all the Ballendian bloodlaws, but I thought appearances were important to a lady's honor."

"We must move quickly; you've only ten more days to your leave."

"Perhaps a walk along the battlements would be less spectacular but just as effective."

"All right," she agreed. "But if I'm to look like a lady with an infatuation, I'd better go inside. I need time to take a bath and prepare."

"My Lady Jacinta is bewitching even with soot on her face," Michael said, taking her hand.

Jacinta gave a pleased laugh. If the conspiracy were distasteful to her, there was no sign of it now.

CHAPTER
6

Jacinta had changed gowns three times and sent the ladies' maids scurrying to find lenses that matched the blue gown before finally resigning herself to wearing the metallic blue already in her eyes. She had known which gown she would wear before she'd even summoned the maids, but she also knew that the right servants' gossip would get more attention than lists of time and frequency of her seeing Michael that the psyche advisers would obtain with great frequency from the brainroom data banks. The maids were probably surprised by Jacinta's behavior, for they'd had to cajole her into dressing specially for dinner just yesterday, but she hoped they would link her unusual behavior to her uncle's unusual dinner guest.

Then she had gone to the wrong informal dining room. She supposed such a mistake would only contribute to more speculation that she was unusually preoccupied, but she would not have worn high-heeled shoes had she known she had to walk all the way to the other side of the castle, and she also would have left her suite earlier. It was frustrating, too, to have to stop to query the castle brainroom for directions and then follow guide lights like a stranger in what was supposedly her own home, but that couldn't be helped. Although she had lived in the castle almost a year

before joining the Corps, she had spent most of that time
confined to her suite in punishment for defying her uncle.

Jacinta had grown up in the relative seclusion of her
father's plantation, not realizing that by the strictest Ballendian standards she was considered wild and unmanage-
able, even if well educated, which, it turned out, was not a
particularly desirable feature in Ballendian females either.
She'd never been considered stubborn or rude back at the
plantation, but neither had she understood that her father
was the scion from the distaff of the Ballendian royal house
and that her bloodline was envied by many Ballendians,
her uncle among them. She had navigator genes, all the
royals did, and they were not dependent on others to plug
into the brainjars for them. As a result, they didn't suffer
from misinterpretations of the data. When you could plug
in yourself, you knew everything about the data, how it was
gathered and why, and most importantly, its limitations.
The percentages imposed on the data were for the benefit
of people who couldn't plug in for themselves and who had
to hire someone who could. They couldn't see all the *what
if's* that a navigator could, and at best they were limited by
their hired navigator's ability to condense, summarize, and
then to communicate these pitiful abstractions by word of
mouth. It was certainly to her advantage now. She knew
exactly the limits of the data her uncle was working from,
and it was fairly easy to maneuver in such a way as to
reinforce the data. Like knowing exactly how he would
expect a love-struck but rebellious niece to act.

By the time she reached the dining room, a niche she
never knew even existed behind the waterfall on the third
level of the atrium, her uncle and cousins were already
seated at the table with their guest, and all had to rise
for her. Michael towered over her uncle and cousins, and
even though she wore high heels, he towered over her. The
only empty chair was next to Cosimo, which made her
sigh. Michael shrugged slightly, which she took to mean
he'd had no choice in the seating. He didn't understand
that her preference in seating had nothing to do with their

conspiracy. She slipped into the empty chair, and the men sat down. Some things she would never be prepared for, no matter how many times she plugged in.

Her uncle had dressed casually in Ballendian tunic top and trousers of homespun silk. The lightweight strength suited his preference for comfort without offending his sense of masculinity. "I'm glad you decided to join us after all," her uncle said, glaring, for he didn't tolerate tardiness well.

"I'm sorry, Uncle Ramon," she said, bowing her head slightly. It was common courtesy for Ballendian women to keep their eyes downcast when speaking to men, a harmless gesture of respect she'd always been taught, though secretly she believed it was so that men could stare openly at her bosom, which they didn't do in the Corps, where the custom of lowering eyes was not practiced. She hated having to remember to behave like a Ballendian female, as her uncle wished, but at least tonight there might be some gain in doing so.

Her uncle signaled the servants to begin serving the meal, which had been suspended in a portable stasis chamber immediately after being prepared, then brought to the dining room. It was, she'd learned aboard *Ship Lisbon*, not without considerable drain on the power kettles, one that military conservancy of power did not permit, not even in the officers dining room.

"You know our guest, Ensign Jivar?" her uncle asked.

"Yes, of course," she said. "We served together on *Ship Lisbon*."

Michael smiled nervously. He was sitting stiffly in the chair across from her, looking somehow out of place. It wasn't his attire; his Corps dress grays with the rust-colored epaulets were appropriate almost anywhere. She decided it was his expression, which lacked the easy look of confidence she'd learned to expect from him in the tundra. It made her wonder what had transpired between him and her kinsmen before she arrived. "My lady looks lovely in clothes," he said, no doubt trying to be gallant despite being uncomfortable in this setting.

"You mean you saw her without clothes?" said Anselem, her other cousin, who was still a youth, and just now, wide-eyed.

"No, of course not," Jacinta said quickly. She could see that Michael only now realized he'd stumbled over his words, and from the look on his face he was uncertain how to correct the situation. She wasn't sure how much he knew about Ballendian proprieties, though she thought that by now he understood how seriously some Ballendian families—especially her family—upheld them. "He means that he has never seen me in civilian clothes before," she said matter-of-factly. "We always wear our uniforms on *Ship Lisbon*." Jacinta stole a glance at her uncle, who was frowning thoughtfully.

"Then he should have said what he meant," Anselem said, refusing the platter the servant was offering so that he could look reproachfully at Jacinta.

Jacinta refused to lower her eyes for Anselem, which infuriated him.

"Father, look at her!" he said. "She's doing it again."

"Anselem, calm down," her uncle said. "We must all be patient with Jacinta while she is recovering from the Corps, not to mention her ordeal at the hands of those knaves."

Jacinta saw Cosimo raise his eyebrows. Cosimo knew how much his father hated Jacinta's spurning custom, and that she was far too clever merely to be experiencing a momentary lapse in what was expected of her. Secretly, she smiled. Her uncle, at least, was behaving in a predictably indulgent fashion.

Michael had not said another word. He ate dutifully, looked uncomfortable. She couldn't blame him; he was probably worried enough about selecting the right utensil without also worrying about slips of the tongue and her bratty cousin. She tried smiling at him to set him at ease, but that just made him stare at her, his face unreadable. Too bad she hadn't thought to let him know that her uncle was sure to be predisposed to forgive any faux pas he might make.

Jacinta supposed they had been seated opposite one another because the psyche advisers had suggested that seeing each other would be more helpful at the early stages of a romance than being able to touch each other under the table. Being Ballendian men, the psyche advisers would assume Jacinta would be more receptive to a conservative approach from a suitor, like their own daughters, or at least as they hoped for their own daughters. The problem was that it was going to be hard to ignore Cosimo, the heir apparent, whose knee was touching hers.

"You're done with the Corps now, aren't you, Jacinta?" Anselem asked, though he knew the answer very well. He was toying with the food on his plate, not looking at Jacinta, so that he would not have to feel ashamed when she would not look away.

"Yes," she said. She turned in her chair so that she could move her leg away from Cosimo, but he had such damn long limbs, she wasn't successful.

"What a shame for the Corps," Michael said, looking up, as if surprised. "Navigator genes are so rare that any who leave are missed, but in your case the Corps is losing a courageous ensign, too."

"Are you talking about Jacinta?" Anselem asked.

The little brat was going to dominate the table talk if she didn't do something. "I wasn't the brave one," she demurred. "It was Michael who dispatched the knaves."

"Did you burn them?" Anselem asked. "How many were there? I didn't know anything about any knaves. Why did you . . . no, I mean how'd you save Jacinta?"

"I didn't do anything that any Corpsman wouldn't have done in my place," Michael said. "It was them or us, and as things turned out, it was them."

"He makes it sound easy," Jacinta said, "but if he weren't the marksman he is, I'd probably be dead. Or worse."

Her uncle looked at her, shocked.

"I was very frightened," Jacinta said, biting her lip, hoping now that she hadn't made him too curious about the incident.

Michael shrugged. "You didn't cry," he said.

"That's not necessarily something a Ballendian lady would be proud to admit," Cosimo said, "but I suppose the Corps wouldn't like it if she had."

"We are proud that the Corps is pleased with Jacinta," her uncle said. "Not many Ballendian women can make the transition from domestic civilian life to a military one. It could not have been easy. Returning to civilian life again should be a much easier transition."

"I've learned a lot in the Corps," she said. Oh, yes. Quite a lot, she thought.

"Sometime I would like to know more of what you've learned," Cosimo said, his fingers rubbing the inside of her thigh.

"Cosimo!" she said sharply. Everyone except Cosimo stared at her in surprise.

Cosimo laughed, but he withdrew his hand and blotted his lips with the napkin. "It's the navigator genes," he said. "Makes them peculiar."

"You have the genes, too?" Michael said, as if it were an innocent question.

Cosimo shook his head and resumed eating.

"You, then?" Michael asked Anselem.

It was Jacinta's turn to be nervous, for Michael, she was sure, was not probing blindly. He looked like he had when the officers were dithering about. Confident. Just making what happened happen as he willed, but somehow not seeming to.

"No," Anselem said. "Jacinta got them from her father, and he's no relative of ours."

"Navigator genes are a curse," Cosimo added, sullenly, jealously.

"Really?" Michael picked up the correct fork and stabbed a morsel of tender meat. "The Corps values people who have navigator genes very highly. I've noticed they treat

navigators and pilots as a kind of blessing. I should think
you would, too. After all, where would the Consortium
be if there were no navigators to pilot starships? Not to
mention your needing brainroom jockeys as much as a
starship does."

Jacinta stole a glance at her uncle. Michael was treading
on dangerous ground, likely offensive to her uncle because
he would have loved his sons to have had his niece's
potential because then they could have strengthened his
position in the Consortium. But her uncle was unruffled.

"Not here on Earth," he said. "And if the Consortium
were not here, then Earth wouldn't have anything to help
deal with The Cold."

"And how does that go?" Michael asked, adding, "I've
been away for several years. Is there any progress?"

Jacinta breathed easily again, and started to eat.

"There are a number of new studies you might be interested in seeing," her uncle said. "We've learned a great deal
about how the glaciers progress."

"Yes, I would be very interested in seeing those studies,"
he said.

"They're in the brainjars," Anselem said. "Just ask for
information on The Cold."

"I didn't realize I'd have access to your household com-
puters," Michael said.

"Not privileged access like ours," Anselem said, "but
information on The Cold is available to guests and ordin-
aries."

"Tell me, have there been any proposals on how to stop
the ice from growing?"

Lord Santos shook his head without looking up.

"I thought not," Michael said.

The food stuck in Jacinta's throat. Michael had over-
stepped again, and Cosimo was retrieving his napkin from
the floor and pulling her dress up over her knee as he
bent over.

"The knowledge of how to stop the glaciers will come,
too," her uncle said easily. "But of course by now you know

that the Consortium's first goal is to understand how and
why this horrible ice age has progressed so quickly. Once
we know that, what to do about it will become clear."

"You've been studying it for forty years," Michael said.

"That hardly seems very long compared to the two thousand years it has been in existence." Her uncle smiled.
"You're a native, and your impatience is understandable,
but when we decide what to do to stop The Cold, you can
be confident it will work."

"The Consortium used to talk about reversing The Cold,
not just stopping it."

"The Hudson Ice Sheet has grown," Jacinta said, and
when her uncle frowned at her, she added defiantly, "the
place where I landed the shuttle should have been miles
from the ice, but we could see it, right there. That was
in Kansas. But even here in the Illinois areas I can tell
when I look out from my balcony that the ice is closer."

"The winters have been unusually wet," he replied, as if
that were enough to discount her observation.

"It'll be great when I can go tobogganing right from
the terrace," Anselem said. "Do you like to toboggan?"
he asked Michael.

"I've never tried it with a real sled, but I used to like
sliding down the hills on a piece of packing board when I
was a boy."

"Packing board?" Anselem said. He had resumed eating
in earnest, summoning the servants back for second help-
ings of his favorite dishes. "Didn't you have a sled?"

Michael shook his head. "No, just packing board."

"Wouldn't that get soggy after a while?"

Michael smiled. "After a short while, as a matter of fact.
But we didn't know any better. We just sledded as long as
it lasted."

"I've never seen anyone use packing board on the toboggan runs," Anselem said doubtfully.

"My friends and I didn't use the same runs. Ours were
usually at the glacial terminus. We couldn't use the parks

the Consortium carved out of the ice sheet each winter for Cradle residents."

"You're an iceman?" And when Michael nodded, Anselem turned to his father, looking aghast.

"He saved your cousin's life," his father said sternly. "And he's a Corpsman."

Anselem considered a moment. "I'm going to be an officer in the Corps," he said seriously. "I already have two sponsors, Lord Alcalde, who lives back on Ballendo, and Admiral Meklan, who is stationed right here on Earth. Who are your sponsors?"

"My sponsor is dead; I have none."

Anselem smiled. "Then I'll outrank you very quickly, won't I?"

Michael nodded. "Probably."

Anselem seemed relieved.

"But you won't outrank me," Jacinta reminded him. It was mean to do, but he was being rude, even for Anselem.

"You are a retired navigator. And when I come home to visit, you'll have to treat me with proper respect, because I'd be fully grown and an officer in the Corps, and you are nothing but a woman."

Jacinta was not going reopen that argument, not now. But she savored the thought of meeting the brat in uniform, say in ten years. Just now, she wanted desperately for something about this dinner to go right. "Don't you go to Youth Corps or something this summer?" she asked Anselem.

"I leave tomorrow," Anselem said matter-of-factly, then added proudly, "But not for the one here on Earth. Father's sending me to Ballendo."

Her uncle smiled indulgently at his youngest son. "As much for the Corps exposure as to reinforce in him what we are and who we are," he explained.

Anselem didn't need any reinforcement, nor did Cosimo. Her older cousin's hand was on her thigh again. The bastard seemed to sense that she didn't want a scene tonight. Seething, she put her napkin on the table and pushed her chair back.

"Are you finished already, sweet cousin?" Cosimo said. "You've hardly touched your food."

"I've had enough," she said icily, and dug her fingernails into his wrist. Cosimo just smiled. The more she gouged him, the more he smiled.

"How did you kill those knaves?" Anselem asked Michael. "Knives or guns?"

Michael was staring at Jacinta, and Anselem had to ask him again.

"Um, both," Michael said. "I mean, one with a knife and the other with a gun."

"You aren't wearing marksman bars," Anselem said. "I can turn a teacup into slag at fifty meters. I'm working on seventy-five."

Cosimo's hand must be bleeding on her dress, Jacinta thought, but he still smiled at her, mocking her.

"Mine was a lucky shot," Michael said, sitting taller in his chair. "Jacinta, what . . ."

"Uncle Ramon, I need some air," Jacinta said abruptly, and she stood up, backing away from the table, out of Cosimo's reach. "May I be excused?"

"Of course, my dear. Are you all right?"

"I'm fine. I just need some fresh air. I'll just go onto the parapets."

Michael stood up. "May I fetch a wrap for you?" he asked.

In her eagerness to be away from Cosimo, she almost said no, but she caught herself. "Yes, thank you. That would be very nice." She looked at her uncle again, belatedly thinking of his approval. "Would it be all right if Michael brought me a shawl?"

"Yes, that's fine. Go. Go, go, go."

She dashed out the door, not hearing whatever else it was that Michael was saying. At the end of the corridor, she ducked into the shimmer of a lift shaft, which took her to the highest level inside the atrium, where the waterfall began its contorted journey to the pools below. She used to like to look out over the atrium to see the water played by the shimmering energy fields that artfully interrupted the fall with suspended pools and cascades, but no longer. Every extravagance was symbolic of her uncle's wealth and power—power over her. She burst through the outside door so fast it barely had time to dilate. Then on the parapets, she huddled against the battlements, her skin still crawling with the feel of Cosimo's hand. She breathed deeply, wishing she could scream but knowing she didn't dare because it would be heard, even if only through mechanical ears, but it would set off an alarm that would bring guards on the run. It was icy cold out here, but anything was better than having her cousin's hands on her, even being cold and alone.

By the time Michael arrived with her shawl, she was shivering. He said her name softly, and when she didn't answer, he came up behind her and wrapped the shawl and his arms around her.

"I don't think your cousins like me," he finally whispered.

"You may find this hard to believe, but they were on their very best behavior," she said.

"Even Cosimo?" Michael asked.

"You saw?" she said.

"I saw how you were reacting," he said. "It took everything I had not to yank him out of his chair and bash his face in."

Surprised, Jacinta turned so she could see his face. He still had his arms around her, and he looked angry. "We shouldn't be talking like this," she said.

"I know," he said, "ears everywhere."

"And you shouldn't be holding me," she said.

"I know."

"Then let go."

He dropped his arms to his sides, looking at her as if he greatly regretted it.

"Why couldn't you appeal to your uncle?"

"You don't understand," she said hotly, "so let's just not talk about it."

"I understand how upset you are, and that you don't get that way without cause."

Jacinta shook her head. How could she explain that her uncle made light of her accusations, and that for all his outward appearance of propriety, he wouldn't do anything about Cosimo's unwanted attentions because then he'd have to admit his own were also unwanted. Even if Michael believed her, there was nothing he could do about it.

"Jacinta . . . ?"

"Let's walk," she said, hugging the shawl to her chest and hurrying down the parapet. The breeze was bracing, but her feet hurt and her knees were trembling. As soon as she found a place where the breeze was cut off, she stopped. They were standing between two massive laser cannons.

"These are the ones they fired on the resistance troops when my father was a young man." Michael leaned up against one of the big guns, eyeing her. "Do you know how many kettles it takes to fire up lasers of this size?"

She shook her head. "A lot, I suppose."

"If they used all the cannons, it would dim Cradle City," he said, gesturing to the glittering lights above them penetrating a mile into the sky.

"We don't use Cradle's kettles," she said. "We have our own. Most of them are bigger than *Ship Lisbon*'s, but just as efficient."

Michael looked down the side of the castle wall, then turned to look at the highest point, which was still one hundred and fifty feet above them. "This castle is massive, but not big enough to accommodate coils and kettles," he said.

"They're below," she said.

"Below?" he said, interested but puzzled. "There's nothing but City Under below. The castle is on the lowest level of Cradle City."

"Beneath City Under," she said.

"That's solid rock."

"Not so solid as most people think," she said, sighing because she thought she should speak again, pretend again that everything was all right. "There's an ancient cavern beneath the castle. I used to go there to see the ruins. It's bigger than the ones in Omaha."

"What kind of ruins are in the cavern?"

"Probably the best-preserved ones on the planet," she said. Yes, she thought. This was better. Michael seemed genuinely interested, and the ruins, though not well known, were not secret and did not make her sweaty to talk about. "My uncle let the University of Ballendo's archaeology department excavate some of it just before they installed the new kettles. They said they date from the Holocaust of 2310."

"And I bet they carried off our archaeological treasures to Ballendo, too, didn't they?"

"Where would you have put them?" Jacinta asked, surprised by his sudden vehemence. "Earth's best museums are already covered with mile-thick glaciers; you people didn't bother to save them. In another hundred years or so this area will be under ice, too. We've saved those artifacts for all humankind."

"Well, at least you don't pretend the Consortium's going to keep its promise to reverse The Cold," Michael said bitterly.

"This is not a good conversation for us to be having," Jacinta said sharply.

"Why? Because you . . ." He caught her meaning mid-sentence, nodded sheepishly, and gestured for her to walk on. Hurting feet or no, she decided to walk.

A moment later he took her hand and pulled her gently from the parapet walk to a narrow staircase that led to a cantilevered balcony.

"Careful," he said when she tried to pull her hand from his to take the railing. "The steps are steep." He winked, and she smiled to indicate she understood they were performing for the benefit of mechanical ears and hidden observers.

She let him steady her on the steps, and then lead her to the battlement, where she again tried to withdraw her hand.

He wouldn't let go, and he pretended not to see her angry glance.

"The stars must be out in great number tonight, Jacinta," he said blithely, staring up at the smattering of stars in the nighttime sky. "It's a pity the lights prevent our seeing all of them."

It's all play-acting, she said to herself, and he's only holding your hand. She just couldn't help wishing he would let go, and that the feeling of panic would subside. She felt trapped, like she had by Cosimo's hand.

"They're a sorry lot compared to what we can see out the viewplates of *Ship Lisbon*," he added.

Desperately, she tried to pull away again, and he held fast.

"Perhaps a navigator doesn't feel the same way about the stars," Michael said, turning to look at her for the first time. "What's wrong?"

"Let go," she said.

He released her immediately.

She breathed deeply, clutching the shawl with both hands, willing the panic away. She didn't know how long they had stood there, but it was a very long time.

"Are you all right?" he asked at last.

"Fine now," she said, and it was nearly true. The knots that had formed in her stomach the moment he'd touched her had eased when she told him to let go. The dread of uncontrolled recurrence was not there, as it had been with Cosimo.

Michael turned and put both his hands on the battlements, leaning out and looking away, the slight frown evident around his eyes and mouth.

She leaned out, too, placing her hand on his.

"You sure you want to do that?" he asked. "Or have you decided whatever it was that repulsed you won't rub off?"

"It had nothing to do with you," she said. "I'm sorry if you thought that."

He looked at her, and apparently satisfied that she was telling the truth, he took her hand between his, rubbing it, and then warming it with his breath. The knots in her stomach stayed slack this time and she reveled in the warmth. He turned her hand from its herald side to expose her jack. It was plugged with a tiny blue gem, and he ran his fingers over it. Jacinta shivered. No one had ever touched her jack like that before; it had never occurred to her that it would feel so nice.

"They say that when navigators plug in, they've got all the mnemonics in the ship's brainroom on call in their own minds, just as if it were their own memories," he said.

Jacinta nodded. "Something like that," she said.

"They say you like to plug in, that you even relish it," he said.

"It's true," she said simply. "Does that horrify you?"

"No," he said. "It makes me curious. What's it like?"

Everyone asked sooner or later, and Jacinta shook her head, just as she always did. "You wouldn't understand," she said.

"Probably not," he almost whispered, grinning impishly at her. "But you're supposed to want to try making me understand. I can't believe that starborn women are so different that they don't share intimate secrets with their lovers."

Jacinta bit her lip. She wasn't sure what other starborn women did, but she had never given a thought to what she would talk about when she was with the man she loved, let alone with a man who she was pretending to love. She supposed it must have to do with intimacies, or they wouldn't be so embarrassed when they were caught at it. She'd better try to say something that the psyche advisers could safely repeat to her uncle, or he would think his plan wasn't working at all, and then where would she be? She took a deep breath. "I can guide the ship from planet to moon, star system to star system. The course of every celestial body between my fix point and destination is plotted and corrected for current time as effortlessly as, well, as walking back up the steps would be."

"Not bad," he said, "but it sounds a bit mechanical to me," and Jacinta knew he meant her effort, not what she had said.

"I'm not very good at . . . explaining things," she said unhappily.

"Sure you are," he said. "You've just never done it before, have you?"

She shook her head.

"Come on," he said coaxingly. "Give it a try."

Jacinta looked at him. His eyes were lighter than hers, his skin darker, but for all of that, she knew they were the same inside, each wanting something better for themselves. If she didn't do her part, neither of them would get what they wanted. Jacinta took another deep breath. "You have to imagine that you understand there are millions of equations from which to choose, but that I can feel the ship's energy ration and merely glance at space-time distance to guide the ship safely, and then," she said, "perhaps you would be properly awed."

"I can," he said, "and I am." He raised her wrist to his lips and kissed the jack again, his eyes glinting.

Jacinta wasn't sure if he was playing the part or playing with her. His grin had broadened to an encouraging smile, a wonderful smile that made her feel at the center of his universe. For a moment she remembered that only a few days ago she'd lain down next to this man and that his arms had reminded her of the times she'd fallen asleep in her father's arms back on Bellendo, safe and warm. But that was before she'd returned to Castle Santos and been rudely reminded how unwelcome some touching could be. She pulled her hand away. "We'd best go inside."

CHAPTER
7

It was a day of firsts for Michael. He had slept in the bed of golden feathers, uneasily at first because the feathers were so cloying that he was afraid they'd smother him if he didn't move carefully. But the fitful dozing became more relaxed as he realized that while the feathers redistributed themselves over his torso and limbs, they always fell away from his face. They also gathered in hoards to support his neck or the crook of his back; by morning the feathers seemed to be anticipating his moves. He was so comfortable he hadn't wanted to respond to the morning awakeners, soft chimes tinkling as if stroked by spring breezes.

He had taken a dry shower only because he knew how to operate it. The water bath, having neither pumps nor faucets, would have required that he query the brainroom for operating instructions, and he knew such queries left trails in the brainjars that brainjar jockeys could follow—and laugh at, too, if they were looking for amusement at his expense. He would deal with the bathroom when he had more time, but for this morning he had needed what extra time there was to don the civilian clothes that had appeared in the wardrobe next to his uniform. At least he'd encountered fasteners of this kind before, though he hadn't been quite sure what to do with a swath of cloth that was

longer than he was tall. It might have been a turban or a
sash, but in the end he left it hanging in the wardrobe.

The house monitor had intercepted him as he was head-
ed toward the dining room and redirected him to a nook
beside an indoor waterfall. He hadn't known that the house
monitor could locate him so easily; he had assumed the
eavesdropping and peeping systems Jacinta had told him
about were passive, but he revised that assumption now.
He would need to ask Jacinta to tell him more about the
system's capabilities so that he did not underestimate it
again. Michael also had not known there was a waterfall
inside Lord Santos's castle; it had not occurred to him
that anyone might want a waterfall inside the house, let
alone dine next to one. In his experience waterfalls tended
to be very noisy and damp. He should have guessed the
starborn would not subject themselves to such unpleas-
antness. Even as he and Jacinta exchanged greetings, the
waterfall noises attenuated, and as Lord Santos joined them
with his two sons, warm, dry air wafted away any hint
of mist from the falls. Nearby, a feast had been laid in
the pit of a round table. The breakfasters could see each
other and converse easily while the food rotated within
easy reach for self-serving. This time everyone had arrived
about the same time, and Jacinta had seated herself between
Michael and Anselem before Cosimo realized what had
happened.

"Where's your sash?" Anselem asked Michael as they
sat down.

"Ah, that's what it was," Michael said, reaching across
Jacinta to grab some steaming hot buns before they rotated
away. Jacinta had leaned back and glared at her young
cousin, no doubt angry at him for pointing out that Michael
had failed to wear a sash. Last night Michael had guessed
Anselem to be about eleven years old, but now he noticed
the pubescent fuzz under his nose and realized the slight
stature of the starborn, not to mention the boy's immature
behavior, had thrown off his estimate. He thought he might
be able to jolly him along, and divert Jacinta's attention,

too. "I was afraid it was a turban, and I didn't know how to wrap it if it was."

But Anselem had begun to bristle the second he caught Jacinta's glare. Her uncle had raised one eyebrow and was looking at Jacinta, but she pointedly didn't look at him, no doubt so that she wouldn't have to lower her eyes. She continued glaring at Anselem. Michael couldn't help but admire her defiance, but he wished she could at least pretend not to feel it so strongly. He was counting on her a great deal, perhaps, he thought guiltily, more than he ought.

"No one would wear a turban with cotton jeans," Anselem said, as much to Jacinta as to Michael.

Michael could have left it at that, and it probably would have died. But he felt compelled to pull Anselem's attention away from Jacinta. "My thought exactly," Michael said, "so, of course, I left it in the wardrobe."

"But you're supposed to wrap it around your waist," Anselem said to Michael, but meeting Jacinta's eyes with equal defiance.

"I didn't know that, so I left it in the wardrobe, thank god."

"Thank god?" Anselem said. Anselem turned away from Jacinta to look at Michael. "Why do you say that?"

"Because I can imagine what your reaction would have been if I'd sat down to breakfast with a sash wrapped around my head."

Anselem laughed. "That would have been very funny."

"Not for me," Michael said. He couldn't help thinking that if he had behaved this way to a guest at his father's table, his father would have sent him away to be dealt with later. Of course, nothing like that had ever happened to him because his imagination conjured sufficient horrors about "later" to preclude his ever wanting to encounter them in the flesh. Jacinta's little cousin had no such reservations. "I don't like being laughed at."

"You would have deserved it," Anselem said, sensing that he'd been rebuked, however gently.

"Anselem!" Jacinta said sharply.

"Anyone who won't ask the brainroom when he doesn't know how to wear a costume deserves what he gets," Anselem said sharply, defensively.

"Did you know that's a sign of dependency and brainjar addiction?" Michael said, biting into the bun.

"What is?" Anselem said.

Michael chewed the flaky bun, savoring the sweetness, before answering Anselem. "Letting brainjars make decisions about what you wear. Next thing you know, you don't know how to make a decision on your own."

Anselem just shrugged. "I don't believe that. Even if it were true, we'd be better off. Brainjars make better decisions than people do because they are so much smarter."

"Anselem, brainjars aren't smart at all, not like people are," Jacinta said. "Brainjars are nothing but circuits that are on or off, positive or negative, yes or no."

Anselem shook his head stubbornly. "I've seen the brainroom masters when they plug in; they know everything."

"No," Jacinta said. "They have access to a lot of information, almost like having encyclopedias and experts' manuals always turned to the right page, but it's still processes and systems between them and the information, and even the masters are not infallible. Sometimes, even though they can see the whole system and understand how the information is stored, it just isn't enough. They still make mistakes."

"You're just saying that because you can and I can't," Anselem said.

"I can what?" Jacinta said, absently buttering a toasted grainstick.

"Plug in," Anselem said, the bitterness in his voice unmistakable.

"Are you still wearing jacks, Jacinta?" her uncle said, speaking for the first time.

"Yes, Uncle," she said demurely. Not only had Jacinta lowered her eyes, but she'd lowered her head as well. At least she had the good sense not to defy her uncle openly.

Her uncle's lips twitched. "I thought we agreed that it was wisest to have them removed promptly."

"We did," Jacinta said, eyes still downcast.

"Then why haven't you had it done?"

"I just . . . forgot to make the arrangements," she said lamely.

"I can do that for you," Anselem said sweetly.

"Don't you need to pack, Anselem?" Jacinta said, meeting the youngster's gaze again, which infuriated him.

"I'm packed and ready, so I have plenty of time to make an appointment for you at the clinic," he said.

"Anselem, may I drive you to the Port Authority?" Michael interjected, regretting now that he had alienated him. Still, for Jacinta's sake and the sake of their mission, he had to try. "I've never been to the civilian side of the Port Authority; I'd like to see it."

"I don't like iceman drivers," Anselem said sourly. "Can't understand them half the time."

"Can you even pilot a notar?" Cosimo asked suddenly, as he exchanged a glance with his father. "Anselem's baggage won't fit into a gyro."

"Of course he can pilot a notar," Jacinta said before Michael could say anything. She pinched his knee when he started to protest. "What time must we leave?"

"No one said you could go," Anselem said, "or him either, for that matter."

"You must leave by ten o'clock," Lord Santos said. His smile was condescending. "Jacinta can show Michael how to check out a notar from my tethers. And I believe she knows the way to the Port Authority and back."

Michael nodded, Jacinta sighed, and Anselem continued eating in deliberate silence.

So Michael had found himself piloting a notar, which he had never done before. Jacinta had coached Michael admirably so he could get the craft safely from the tetherlot at the edge of her uncle's holdings into the commercial air corridor, where Cradle Command's brainjars took over piloting the craft above the tiaga to the Port Authority down south.

"You explain things quite well," Michael said pointedly when he could finally relax. They were gliding smoothly, the graceful rotating wing pulling its load swiftly past the beacons on the glidepath.

"I thought you said you could pilot a notar," Anselem said, the sneer in his voice plain.

Michael cut off the first response that welled. "I must have forgotten a great deal," he said.

"You never knew how," Anselem said flatly. "And you," he said, tapping Jacinta on the shoulder, "deliberately lied to my father. And he let you. I don't know why, but he let you change the topic from getting your jacks removed to taking me to the Port Authority. Cosimo cooperated. Why?"

Michael had noticed that, too, and hoped it meant that Cosimo was privy to Lord Santos's plan. The elder son was a member of his private advisory board, so his knowing made sense. He hoped it would also curb his unwanted attentions toward Jacinta. Obviously, Anselem had not been informed; he was as rude and direct as ever.

"Oh, Anselem. You're always looking for an argument. Must we now, too? You'll be gone for so long, I'd hate to think that the last thing we did together was argue."

"You're trying to change the subject again," Anselem said. "Father's not here to take your side. Answer me!"

"Are you jealous, Anselem?" Michael asked. "Angry, perhaps, that your father and brother didn't take you to the Port Authority?"

"Iceman, I have to tolerate you because you are my father's guest. But for you to presume to analyze my motives is doubly insulting, first in assuming that you can distract me from my questions, and then in believing that you have any insight into my character at all. Now I'll thank you to be quiet and let my cousin answer my question."

Silently, Michael reminded himself not to underestimate Anselem again. He might be spoiled and immature, but he wasn't stupid.

"Jacinta, I'm waiting."

"I've forgotten what the question was," Jacinta said lightly. "Now hush while I help Michael disengage from traffic
control. We've arrived."

"Jacinta, I'll be of age when we next see each other,"
Anselem said. "You'll rue the day."

Jacinta smiled tightly. "We'll see," she said.

"Jacinta, help!" Michael said. The notar was gaining
rapidly on a pair of gyros in the glidepath, and a red light
was flashing on the control panel.

"Push the nose down and power up," she said, "and ease
into the right-branching air corridor."

They swung swiftly past the gyros and followed the corridor into a tetherlot. Michael glanced at Anselem in the
heads-up display; the youngster was sitting with his chin in
his hands, his eyes narrow with anger. Michael almost felt
sorry for him; he'd been left out of an adult conspiracy, and
he knew it. The rage was barely under control, trembling
beneath the surface of cool anger. It occurred to Michael
that if the boy could sustain such anger, Jacinta had better
be safely in the Corps of Means when Anselem came of
age. He was only a boy now, both small in stature and
without resources to be threatening on his own, but when
that changed, watch out. He seemed more alert and a lot
more confrontive than his elder brother and father, and he
just might be more volatile, too.

A baggage handler arrived the instant they tethered the
notar, whisking Anselem's trunks out of the notar's little
cargo compartment and disappearing even before the little
wheeled ferry that came for them started rolling. Anselem
remained silent, not even giving him or Jacinta reproach-
ful glances. They might not have been there for all that
Anselem seemed to care.

The civilian side of the Port Authority holdings included
a terminal big enough to accommodate pods that permitted
simultaneous loading of passengers through the open sides
and their luggage, which was stowed beneath the transparent floor. Anselem stepped on board the pod at his assigned

seat, glanced through the floor to check that the cargo handlers had stowed his trunks, then stepped off again, brushing past Michael and Jacinta as if they were not there. He sat down at a table in the long-side cafe where everyone else waited. Jacinta sat down, too, but Michael decided to walk down the rows of pods and cafes, or was it just one enormous cafe? The architecture, even to his unpracticed eye, was far more expansive than anything he'd seen on the starborn's homeworlds. But then he had to remind himself that even the homeworlds' facilities were quite old compared to what the Consortium had built for starborn comfort here on Earth. And the Port Authority's expansion of the civilian side had been made while he was away, and no doubt paid for with the sale of antiquities found in such abundance here on Earth. Too bad that Earthlings couldn't enjoy it, too.

With the exception of Michael, the people in the cafe were starfarers all. They were mostly small, very white-skinned after the long, snowy winter on Earth, coiffured and dressed in every possible fashion, for it was *the* fashion to dress provincially for the homeworlds, though not necessarily for one's own homeworld. Starfarer crowds had a common character of dignity, manifested by their quiet but deliberate way of doing everything from walking and talking to gazing at him (no doubt because he was so tall) calmly and steadily. They looked at Michael like a herd of beautiful white musk-oxen might look as he strode through their pasture, peaceful, secure, and only mildly curious. It was getting harder for him to hate them, at least these people, who, if not innocent, were at least indifferent to him.

Later, after Anselem had been seated in the pod along with the other passengers, passglass curtains lowered over the open sides, and the pod moved easily across the terminal floor, following a silvery track that was flush with the polished stone islands amidst a virtual sea of blue carpeting. Once Anselem's pod was out on the tarmac where the orbitjumper waited, Jacinta waved to him. He didn't return the wave. He just stared at her.

"Good riddance, you little brat," she muttered. Calmly, she took Michael's arm, and equally calmly, she gave her cousin a final wave. But when she looked at Michael and said, "Let's get the hell out of here," her voice cracked.

"Are you all right?" he asked.

She shook her head as they started walking.

"At least he won't be at meals anymore," Michael said.

"Cosimo will be," she said. "The meals are always the worst." She laughed tightly. "I should be grateful. If the meals were not the worst, it could be even more horrible."

"What's so horrible, Jacinta?" Michael asked, genuinely puzzled and very worried. "I have seen how disagreeable they can be, pigheaded, and even patronizing, but I also see that you're more than a match for them, smarter, more clever, stronger willed. And it antagonizes them. I don't think that's wise."

"Not *wise*!" She shrieked. "You don't know what you're talking about. The horror is that they can't lose. And even when I win, I can lose because it just makes them all the more angry with me. Sometimes I wish I could be the kind of woman they want me to be, just so that I could eat a meal without getting knots in my stomach. I've tried not talking, but then Cosimo . . ." Her voice trailed off.

"What about Cosimo?" Michael asked, the look on her face causing a sinking feeling in his stomach.

Jacinta shook her head as they stepped into a lift shaft that took them up to the tetherlot level. She tightened her grip on his arm and smiled up at him. "It doesn't matter," she said. "Not now. You're something of a prince, coming to take me away from my evil step-family."

"A prince? Me?" Michael said, confused.

"Didn't you ever watch the fairy tales on the holos or read them on a vid?"

Michael shook his head. He wasn't even quite sure what a fairy was, although he was dimly aware that they were as mythical as trolls.

"Well then, let's go to the Cradle City to buy you some fairy tales."

"Cradle City? I don't know. Wouldn't your uncle object?"

"Probably, but come on, Michael. Where's your sense of adventure?"

She looked so eager that he couldn't refuse, even though it occurred to him that he might be playing fast and loose with proprieties. But he decided it couldn't be any more improper for him and Jacinta to drive home unescorted than to go to the city. Unescorted was unescorted, no matter what the destination, and Lord Santos had known that they would be alone when he allowed them to drop off Anselem at the Port Authority. If they were supposed to be romantically involved, they'd have to have *some* time alone. Even Lord Santos knew that. Michael couldn't very well take Jacinta Renya to the places icemen took their girlfriends, though in a way, he longed to do just that. He dismissed the thought. Cradle City would have to do.

Cradle City was another first. As they approached in the notar, the city looked to Michael as it always had, fantastical with its horizontal planes looking like they floated on tethers, though Michael knew full well they were energized pylons and pillars, not tethers at all. The mile-high city was not entirely self-supporting but dependent on the energy of the kettles and coils that formed the central core on which the city spiraled, like graceful branches and leaves. The structure defied gravity, literally, held up by antigravity architecture powered by the central core. Except, of course, for Castle Santos, which had its own coils and kettles, somewhere beneath City Under.

He had spent some winters in City Under, ones when two-hundred-mile-an-hour winds swept the ice sheets clean of even the starborns' melts. The tundra offered little resistance to the winds, and those who could abandoned their huts until spring, basking in the heat Cradle City radiated. But Michael never had been in Cradle City itself, never known that what had looked to him like jewels when he had seen them from the ice sheet were spires and pinnacles of buildings that even up close seemed to be made of crystal and silver.

"Mind the drop zone," Jacinta said, pointing out the shimmering column of air that would have taken them down several hundred feet into a residential tier. He merged right, with the help of the notar's traffic controller, slowly circumnavigating the city in a counterclockwise air corridor at the edge of the third tier, almost one hundred feet above the ground.

Spirals of glistening-white gyropaths and shimmering drop shafts laced the city. A few sleek windshots darted through air corridors Michael could not quite discern, which made him glad he was in the tiny notar with no tail rotor to worry about, and equally glad to have Jacinta's skilled instructions.

Within Cradle were sectors and enclaves, some favoring the builders' homeworld architecture, others packed with entertainments, as well as a few that were isolated, like the castle at the southeastern edge on the lowest tier of the city. On the far south side, where there was a great deal of sunshine to be had when it was not snowing, several tiers were latticed with open skywalks and drop shafts and lift shafts. On the north side, the city was in a shadow of its own making most of the day, where only a few buildings had open-air balconies and all the skywalks were enclosed. Jacinta directed him to a tether for the notar, a shelf on the northern edge, where acres of notars and gyrocraft stood in neat rows while their owners went about their business in the city.

That Jacinta was a necessary guide became evident the moment they stepped out of the notar. There were moving walks and short-walk portals to contend with, both of which he'd heard of but had never encountered, not even on Whitney Planet, and certainly not on Dolphinia. The concept of moving walks was ancient, and he had no difficulty navigating among the three or four parallel strips when he wanted to increase or decrease the speed of his journey. But short-walk portal technology was less than one hundred years old. The grand old cities on Whitney Planet could not easily be retrofitted with them, but they'd been planned into Cradle City, which had been built all new some miles from the glacial terminus. Even after the third time now, it still seemed magical to him to step through the portals and find himself a half mile farther along the way in an eyeblink. There were tall trees here, half-recognizable, like red spruce in full pink candle and weeping beech as luminescent as lightning bugs, a forest of genetically manipulated trees right in the middle of the city. There were even small animals living among the more heavily forested areas, shy, deerlike creatures and bolder squirrels, and an array of exotic birds that tantalized the eye with a flash of color on the wing.

"I thought there was a vid shop here," Jacinta said, letting go of his arm to look around behind them. The area had some grassy expanses lined with neat rows of flowers. "I think I'm all turned around; it's been a long time since I was here," she added apologetically.

There were no shops, but there was a little cafe perched on the edge of nothing, with real waiters scurrying three dimensionally among tables that seemed to be floating. For a moment he wasn't sure if the cafe were a tiny zero-gee zone or if magic just reigned in Cradle City.

"This way, Michael," Jacinta said from behind him.

The spell seemed a diabolical one when a surge of people separated him from Jacinta long enough to sweep him through one portal and her through another. He turned around to walk back through the portal going in the opposite direction, only to realize as he stepped through that there had been *two* more portals he could have chosen from, and obviously the one he had chosen was the wrong one, for the magical cafe was nowhere to be seen. He was standing in the middle of a nearly deserted plaza, a brook bubbling out of crystal-clear latticework underfoot. A quick look at the city tiers above him told him he was not even on the same level as the cafe, and was now facing west. Obviously, short-walk portals did not take you just straight ahead but also up or down, too. There were several out-going portals on either side of the brook, the arches bright yellow, red, and green. He was fairly sure the one that had brought him here had been orange, so it was not obvious to him which to select for a return. If there was a key to the color coding, it was not plain to him.

Now what? He shoved his hands in his pockets, but took them out quickly when he felt himself drawing curious stares. Starfarers didn't stand around with their hands in their pockets; they'd never had cold hands long enough to develop such a habit. Earlier he had seen flower-filled terraces and nooks by the walks where people sat on benches, but this place was barren, a plaza of some sort with nothing but the short-walk portals and some connecting skywalks bridging the way to nearby buildings.

He stood for a long time just studying the portals, looking for some clue to figuring out their destination. There had to be one, or some kind of key. He stared at the arches; they were bright, almost luminescent colors, but there was no writing or symbols or anything resembling signage, and no brainjar coolers or vocal query sensor.

Michael had just made up his mind to ask the next person to come out of the portal how to get back to the floating cafe—surely the cafe would be recognizable by description, even if he didn't know its name or location—when a Planetary Guard wearing a Consortium sash strolled off the north skyway. Great! Just what he needed. A stick. He looked at Michael with interest. Michael was doing nothing, but he knew that simply by standing in the center of a plaza full of short-walk portals he was behaving peculiarly. He also knew better than to ask a stick for directions, not while wearing civilian clothes and towering over the guy by a head. He'd spent enough time in the Corps to know that those attached to the Consortium Guard were the same ones that patrolled City Under and the ice sheet, their duties regularly rotated. A stick was a stick, and a stick would know an iceman when he saw one. With the guard's first step toward him, Michael turned and walked purposefully toward the southbound skyway. He had no idea where it would take him; he didn't much care, as long as it was away.

He stopped walking when he heard Jacinta call his name for a second time. Turning back toward the plaza, he watched her wave and run toward him. The guard had halted, too, his foot on the southbound skywalk. He stepped aside to let Jacinta pass.

"Thank goodness you didn't take another short-walk," she said, sounding breathless. "If I'd lost you and had to go home alone, my uncle would have been furious."

Almost possessively, she took his arm. He clamped his fingers over hers, equally possessive. The guard seemed less curious now, and Michael breathed easier.

"Let's find a cafe," Jacinta said, looking back toward the portals, the plaza, and the guard. "Some of them have vids and entertainments."

"Maybe there's one this way," Michael said, pulling her onto the skywalk.

"It'll be faster through the short-walk," she said, but Michael pulled her firmly along the skywalk.

"But . . ."

"No," he said firmly. "I'm not going to risk losing you again in those things."

Jacinta relented with a shrug. "Uncle Ramon would know it was my fault. The psyche advisers wouldn't let him take his anger out on you; they'd worry you'd get frightened away."

"It isn't your uncle that I'm concerned about," Michael said. "It's the Consortium Guards. With my height, they'll look closely at me, and if they notice an icer herald, they just might arrange for me to spend the rest of my leave in the lockup."

"I didn't think of that," Jacinta said.

"Why would you?" he said. "Cradle is a starfarer city, and you're a starfarer."

"Why do I get the feeling you hold that against me?" she asked.

He didn't answer.

Later, in a cafe, when they had run out of things to say about the two fairy tale vids that lay on the table, and while they were sipping something hot and fruity, she repeated the question. "Why do you hate starfarers?"

Her question was so sincere, he couldn't help laughing. "You really don't have a clue, do you?" She frowned, but he shook his head. "Put yourself in our shoes for a minute. People we've hardly even thought about for more than a thousand years come back stronger and in larger numbers than we ever imagined and just . . . steal our resources from us." He gestured helplessly.

"Earth doesn't have any resources," she said. "Everything worth having was used up fifteen hundred years ago."

"There are other resources besides natural ones," he said.

"You mean the antiquities from the glaciers?" And when he nodded, she shook her head vehemently. "Michael, the antiquities in the glaciers are a nonrenewable treasure that belongs to all humanity. Saving antiquities that are revered throughout the galaxy requires galactic cooperation. You Earthlings have nowhere near the resources needed to secure our priceless heritage—and remember, it is *our* heritage, too. If we allow the antiquities of Terran civilization to be destroyed, the whole galaxy will share the loss."

"But there's the difference," he said. "I say it's not yours. Your ancestors left two thousand years ago. Mine stayed. The antiquities are ours, not yours."

"But you don't take care of them. You haven't the resources or knowledge to do it properly," she said reasonably.

"And just because you do have the resources and knowledge, do you think I should be grateful and not resent your interference?"

"Yes," she said with complete sincerity.

Michael sat back in the comfortable chair and took a deep breath. "Jacinta, what is it about Cosimo the repels you?

"What? Why are you changing the subject?"

"I'm not. I saw the effect Cosimo had on you at the table. I think I know what he was doing, what he had to have been doing to have caused you to flee from the table and tremble for an hour thereafter."

Her head jerked up.

"You wouldn't appeal to your uncle because you knew he wouldn't help you. It's you alone against Cosimo, right?"

"What do you think you know?" she said, the drink forgotten in her hand. She looked very pale.

"Look, I'm trying to make a point. Your uncle is well-meaning but blind to . . ."

"My uncle is blind to nothing," she said, almost whispering. "You think he doesn't see what Cosimo is doing? He knows exactly what goes on between Cosimo and me."

Stunned, his point momentarily forgotten, Michael stared at her. Her eyes were angry and defiant, but she had such a tight grip on the teacup Michael was afraid the fragile porcelain would shatter.

"Then why doesn't he put a stop to it?" Michael said.

"Because if he did, then he'd probably have to stop himself, too, don't you think?"

Michael stared at her a second. "Your uncle? Are you sure he . . ."

"Michael, before you utter one more word of doubt, let me tell you that you can't possibly have more doubts than I did for a long, long time. Good god, for years I didn't even know the words to describe it, let alone that it was wrong. I only knew that it felt . . . sickening. I was ashamed and frightened."

"Why didn't you tell someone?"

"You really don't understand," she said, drawing back from him. "Tell them what? There was no way to describe *that*. And to whom? Everyone I was supposed to be able to trust was doing it to me."

Michael swallowed and nodded. He had no idea of what to say.

"I thought it was all my fault," she said. "I was the one who was different. I thought it was because I didn't always remember to lower my eyes and my curtsies were never very good." She shrugged helplessly, her eyes brimming with tears.

"It wasn't your fault. It still isn't your fault." Michael reached across the table to take her hand, but stopped himself. He didn't think his touch would be reassuring to her. He pulled his hand back. "I'm sorry," Michael said, after a long pause. "I thought Cosimo was an annoying groper. I didn't realize what had been going on, nor that it was both of them." His fists were clenched on the table, the point he'd wanted to make about Terran powerlessness paled by the immediacy and personalness of hers. "Jacinta, I don't want to take you back there," he said.

"I've thought of running away," she said, "but I don't know how." She looked a little sheepish. "I mean, I don't think I could run anywhere except right here to Cradle City. I don't know how to blend in anywhere else. You saw me on the tundra; I couldn't build a fire. Until I joined the Corps, it never occurred to me that I could comb my own hair or dress myself. Oh, I did learn, and now I know I can make my way in the Corps. But I can't run away and join the Corps, can I?"

"No, you can't. Not unless we go back to your uncle's castle and play our gambit all the way through," he said.

"Well, there you have it then. Shall we go? It's getting late," she said, shoving her teacup across the table.

Michael grabbed her hand but let it go just as quickly, frightened of touching her. She seemed to understand his hesitation, for she almost smiled as she twined her fingers in his. "There's something you need to know," he said.

"What?"

"That you could run right here in Cradle City. There are . . . people who would pay you if you'd plug in for them, use your jacks to advise them. They would pay you well and keep you safe from your uncle if that's what you wanted. Rogue navigators can just about name their prices."

"Rogue navigator," she said with a wry smile. But she gave a shake of her head. "I'm lousy with politics and palace intrigue," she said. "It took you to see the possibilities of turning my uncle's plan to my advantage. This double cross would never have occurred to me. I just don't think that way. I'd never make it as a rogue."

"Oh, you could do it if you wanted to," Michael said. "But maybe, for a start, you'd like not to be on your own. Maybe for a while I could show you the ropes, as they say. You'd learn quickly."

"Why would you give up your Corps career to become a criminal?" she asked suspiciously.

"Because I don't want to take you home," he said softly. "Not to them." And that was the truth, but it was not the whole truth. There were no limits to the possibilities of what patriots could do with a rogue navigator to guide them through the Consortium's brainrooms.

Jacinta nodded and pulled her hand out from under his. "But you will take me home," she said resolutely. "And you will say nothing of what I've told you and let no hint of it creep into your attitude toward Cosimo or my uncle. I'm not cut out to be a criminal, nor are you. We can have good careers in the Corps. We just have to be patient for another week."

"As you wish, my lady," he said resignedly. But already he was wondering if there was anything short of death that was adequate compensation for what they had done to her. And that was another first for him, to realize that he would do anything for Jacinta, even kill again for her.

CHAPTER
8

Too often, Michael could not sleep. The bed of golden feathers was more comfortable and soothing than any he had slept on in his life, but it did not stop the night terrors. They always started with the sound of magpies quarreling, a distant sound that wouldn't disturb any sleepers but those tuned to it. He could smell the dead coals in his father's fireplace the instant before the sound of heavy footsteps brought him bolt upright in the bed. As he gasped for breath, the little golden filaments sucked the sweat that would be pouring from his body. Then he would sit in the sound-dead room, letting the terror subside until the saturated filaments dropped off and sank beneath fluffy feathers that were dry and warm. He'd get up and shower, knowing that if he tried to sleep, he'd dream again. Instead, he'd prowl the parapet walk, the upper battlement terraces, and the concourse of terraces and gardens at lowest level. It wasn't long before he'd explored the full circumference of Lord Santos's holdings at each of those levels and knew where each big gun was placed along the battlements and which were supported by true bearing walls and which were balanced by the antigravity architecture powered by the kettles. But though he explored every drop shaft and lift shaft, he could find none that led to the caverns where Jacinta had told him the power kettles were. It was possible, he supposed, that they were not accessible from the castle, though if that were the case, they'd have to be accessible from City Under, and that did not seem reasonable to him at all. But for sticks sweeping City Under for icers without heralds or passes, the starborn had no presence there.

Michael had tried querying the brainroom, making many random requests, including reports on The Cold and current fashions, topics he imagined the psyche advisers or even Lord Santos himself would find predictable. His query on power kettles provided a hauntingly familiar and seemingly endless series of schematics and equations relating to the physical properties of kettles and a sketchy description of Cradle City's core of kettles along with tour information. He was beginning to wonder if Jacinta had been mistaken about Castle Santos having its own source of power, almost ready to question her more closely about it, though he loathed the thought of doing that. She would surely remember the conversation someday, and perhaps feel some complicity herself.

Funny, he'd never thought to look up the kitchen's location, though he had noticed that he hadn't seen much of the castle's tactical operations. He'd found the kitchen simply by following his nose, the scent of biscuits baking to be exact, delicious molecules wafting up a lift shaft that was one of many drilled right through the supporting pylons and tethers that held Cradle City aloft. It's what he'd expected when Jacinta mentioned the cavern, but which he couldn't find until he smelled the biscuits. The icers in City Under used the pylons like tree trunks for their winter tents. Years ago there had been attempts to sabotage Cradle City by strapping explosives to the pylons, but the patriots hadn't understood even the basics of the antigrav technology. The destructive energy of the explosives had just discharged into the surrounding shacks and tents. Innocent icers had died by the score. Even if it had been possible to sabotage the pylons and tethers, it occurred to him now that the whole city could fall and not damage what was so cleverly concealed in the vast caverns. He'd searched for concealed terminuses on the lowest tier of the castle, but not for staircases in what he'd thought were pantries.

Beneath the permafrost were the servants' quarters and work areas, the hub of activity that kept the starborn Lord Santos luxuriously comfortable. He found immaculate kitchens and pantries with stores of exotic imports and lockers full of locally grown staples. A cool wine cellar sparkled with personalized decanters from many worlds, the black market value of just one could have kept an icer family fed for six months. Frothing hydro-tanks were only lightly used, but the yeast and algae closets were filled with growth-nubs and catalysts, ostensibly in preparation for winter events when the two-hundred mile-an-hour winds that funneled off the glaciers could ground the fleet for weeks. The same supplies could be used during a siege, though the last one had been before Michael was born, and any of the starborn would scoff at such a notion. Interesting, too, that servants carried foodstuff and supplies up the narrow staircases routinely so that Castle Santos would be prepared for a siege. The stasis serving trays made more sense to him now.

Of great interest to Michael was the energy plant. He found it on the seventh night of his leave. It, too, was in the castle's subterranean level, though not accessible from the work hub. A narrow staircase led off the main passage near Lord Santos's own study in the Santos family suites. The first part of the stairs were formed plasteel, spiraling steeply—a simple but effective deterrent to any starborn who would by nature seek a drop shaft. Below that were more stairs, but these were of rough-hewn stone. There was no guard. Michael knew that castle security was so thorough that only authorized persons and guests could ever gain entry to the castle itself, so apparently they didn't worry too much about who might find the stairs. Human security guards were rarely visible, though from what Jacinta had told him, Michael assumed that almost every room and terrace in the castle was monitored in some fashion.

Below the stone staircase, Michael found a drop shaft to an even lower level. The energizer was personalized to palm prints, but he found the power on. Although it occurred to him that the power might disengage in the presence of an unfamiliar body, he stepped into the drop shaft; he might never have another chance. Apparently once the power was on, it stayed on, for he descended safely.

Even though he knew it had to be huge, the size of the cavern astounded him. It was hollowed out of the white limestone, much bigger than the massive kettles and coils required. The drop shaft had deposited him on a network of polysteel gangways above the kettles. He could see the shimmering columns of other drop shafts between the gangways and the cavern floor. On the far side, he saw the ruins Jacinta had talked about, a four-story building of ancient cube style made of some building material he could not identify. It looked intact.

Below him he could see lights traveling along the control panel, others flashing steadily. The single-beam pipe, the coils, and the housing for the magnets indicated a simple electron-positron collider, yet the placement of magnets looked odd. Then he saw the plasma generator, and realized everything was upsidedown—not what he was accustomed to seeing—because this must be an antimatter kettle. The only sound was the droning hum of pumps, all too quickly interrupted by the sound of footsteps on the polysteel planking. Before Michael could move, a technician came into view, a brainjar canister clipped to his belt to record data from the dials along the gangway that he was absently monitoring. He stopped as he spotted Michael in the periphery of his vision.

"Who are you?" he asked, surprised, not at all pleased.

"Ensign Michael Jivar, a guest of Lord Santos," Michael replied more calmly than he felt.

The technician was dressed like a Corpsman, but with the familiar gray and scarlet sash, indicating he was attached to Lord Santos's personal staff. He was unarmed. Michael looked at the man's wrist for what the herald could tell him, but he didn't recognize it. He knew only that he wasn't dealing with a Ballendian or a technician from one of the Council worlds, which meant he was a fringe worlder, imported talent.

"What are you doing here?" the tech asked.

"I'm a kettle tender on *Ship Lisbon*," Michael said, shrugging slightly. "Professional interest."

"You're out of uniform."

"I'm on leave."

The technician apparently felt no professional kinship to Michael. "Does Lord Santos know you're here?" the tech asked suspiciously.

"No. I couldn't sleep, so I decided to explore the castle. There wasn't any sign to indicate I shouldn't enter."

The technician frowned. "I forgot to disengage the drop shaft. That's the only thing that keeps intru . . ." He shook his head, seemingly embarrassed. "I mean, no one is supposed to be down here unless Lord Santos expressly authorizes them."

"Have you been on Earth very long?" Michael asked, his manner direct now, like the officers used.

The tech shook his head. "I just arrived three days ago." He chanced a glance at Michael's herald; Michael almost smiled because the icer herald would reveal little to a newcomer. He'd assume it was a starborn herald that he wasn't familiar with.

"Since you're a newcomer, I suppose you must be forgiven a breach of etiquette. But if you've disregarded a direct order to disengage the drop shaft as a security measure, that is a matter of great importance and probably consequences," Michael said gravely.

The tech was obviously confused. He had no doubt been briefed on Ballendian etiquette, but was unable to recall any violation of custom in his encounter with Michael, because of course there was none. But having been challenged, he apparently wasn't certain.

"I'm sorry. I . . ." He hesitated, then added, "It's a security measure I'm not accustomed to, sire."

Michael noted with amusement that he had been promoted from sir to sire, which he knew from his own etiquette briefings was completely unnecessary but sure to please most starborn civilians.

"Get accustomed to it fast, or you'll find yourself back in the fringe!"

The tech snapped erect. "It won't happen again, sire."

"I shall personally check to see that it does not," Michael said. He turned abruptly and went back to the shaft, where he lifted to the level above. The power faded behind him, and he hurried up the stone stairs.

The tech would be confused as to his tormentor's identity, but he was not likely to inquire, least of all to Lord Santos. To do so would be to confess his unforgivable oversight, which would no doubt also be listed in the alarm logs, but which Michael knew stood a very good chance of being overlooked as long as someone didn't have reason to check them. He knew from personal experience that going through mountains of data was the last thing anyone did for fun. There was too much, nearly all of it routine, even the exception reporting and alarm logs. Michael had seen enough to know the coils and kettles of Castle Santos were a similar version of the one on *Ship Lisbon*, except that it used antimatter plasma in the beams. The spinning dials and flashing lights were no mystery to Michael. Even the surly chief tech on *Ship Lisbon* had grudgingly admitted that Michael had the "feel of the kettles," as the techs called it. He had spent time with Michael, who amused him by learning what he could and then trying to get a step ahead by studying what was in the brainjars.

Michael ducked through the doorway at the head of the staircase, and slipped silently into the empty corridor. A few steps past Lord Santos's study, the household monitor intercepted him.

"Ensign Jivar," it said softly from somewhere above him. "Lady Jacinta requests that you join her on her terrace. Shall I light the directionals for you? Lady Jacinta believes you have lost your way."

"I was lost," he said carefully, "but I know where I am now. I can find my way from here."

"As you wish," the monitor said.

He continued on down the corridor to the atrium with the waterfall, hurried past the pool to another corridor that led to his suite. The door opened at his approach, and he hurried out through the passglass on the other side. Morning light had barely broken. In the east, the glacier glittered golden pink. Jacinta stood near the railing, a fluffy cloak around her shoulders protecting her against the chill morning air.

"You shouldn't have gone below without permission," she said, not even greeting him first.

"I was curious about the ruins," he said.

"And in satisfying your curiosity, you set off the alarm logs." She was angry, and not just a little. "I know you understand about alarm logs."

Michael shrugged. "Most alarm logs are too long to scrutinize closely."

"This isn't *Ship Lisbon* where everyone who looks at alarm logs is expected to eliminate the innocent alarms before reporting them," she said sharply. "This is Castle Santos, which has a whole new brainroom where they're still trying to perfect the system. Every alarm is investigated."

"I didn't know that," Michael said uneasily. She sounded uncannily like the chief tech when that officer was giving him a dressing down. "If you think it will cause a problem, perhaps I should go talk to your uncle before someone else does. I could explain . . ."

"Not to his satisfaction," she said impatiently. "Don't you realize that the profile of a glitz-struck native who wants to see how starfarers really live is not much different from a terrorist looking for security vulnerabilities?"

Shit! Michael thought. If even Jacinta was making the connection, what were Santos's brainroom masters doing? "So what do we do now?" he asked, knowing there was only one thing that could be done, but afraid that suggesting it himself would be too bold.

"*We* won't do anything," she said. "I've already taken care of it."

"Taken care of it?" he asked, trying to sound as if he couldn't imagine how she could accomplish such a thing, though not without wondering if she'd think him stupid for not knowing.

"I adjusted the entries in the logs."

"You plugged in again?"

"They know I'm doing it, but they think I'm just deafening the ears here on the balcony, which of course I am."

"There was a tech . . ."

"I adjusted his report, too. He'll be surprised when he doesn't get a reprimand for leaving the power on in the drop shaft, but I don't think he'll go asking for one."

"Thanks."

She nodded. "I didn't really want to take the chance of you and my uncle discussing the antiquities in the cavern, especially not who they belong to, and most especially not when there's something more important you ought to be discussing with him."

"Such as?"

Jacinta took a deep breath. She no longer resembled any Corps officer. More like a little girl steeling her courage. "If we're going to go through with this thing, you need to ask his permission for us to marry."

"If?" Michael said, taking her hand in his. Her fingers were warm against his skin. "Are you having second thoughts?"

Eyes downcast, Jacinta shook her head. "The psyche advisers are predicting that there's a fifty percent chance that we've already talked about marriage, so he's half-expecting you to approach him. I just thought it would be best to do that soon, to stay within their expectations."

"I'll talk to him after breakfast," he said.

Jacinta nodded curtly and bit her lip, her eyes still downcast. She wasn't wearing lenses this morning, and her brown pupils were exquisitely soft. Michael hated the lenses that masked their intense, velvety depth and was glad she wasn't wearing them. Yet now there was nothing to mask the sadness.

"What's wrong?" he asked her. When she didn't answer, he lifted her chin with his fingers. This time there was something frantic in her eyes, and he asked again, "What's wrong?"

"What will I do if he refuses?"

"He's not going to say no," Michael said. "He needs this marriage."

"So do I," she said.

"And I," Michael said. "And with all the parties involved wanting the same thing, what can go wrong?"

"Marry the Lady Jacinta? You? Even your asking is an insult, let alone your assuming I would consider it." Lord Santos's voice was brittle, almost hollow.

In a padded chair behind a desk that looked to be carved from agate, Lord Santos twitched, whether from anger or eagerness Michael could not tell.

Michael fought to keep calm. Had Lord Santos changed his plans after all? Or was this an act to keep Michael from realizing he intended to use the couple? If he'd changed the plan, Jacinta had not detected it, so Michael decided he had no choice but to continue to play his part as convincingly as he could.

"Sire, I have a satisfactory future in the Corps of Means."

"You have no future at all in the Corps of Means," Lord Santos said. "Not without a sponsor, you don't. But if you were to marry my niece, you wouldn't lack for sponsors, would you?"

"I don't know, sire. I hadn't thought that far ahead. I'm not asking anything for myself, only that you consider Lady Jacinta's desires."

"Lady Jacinta's best interests, eh? You think I don't understand what a boon such a marriage would be to you, iceman?"

Michael shrugged mildly. "I wouldn't ask for her only for my own sake. You must consider Lady Jacinta's heartfelt desire."

Lord Santos's face darkened and he nodded sourly. "It's

true that a heartsick woman is a burden, and . . . blast her! She can be stubborn enough." Abruptly, he stood up and walked to the far wall, fingering the ancient books on sparkling shelves. Then he paced between the wall and the recording console, finally stopping to put his hands on the console, lowering his head in thought. "If this marriage is her will, I won't interfere," he said, sourly enough.

"Your lack of interference is not enough, sire," Michael persisted.

Lord Santos looked up at him, glowering.

"We want your approval."

"You ask too much, iceman."

"I wouldn't ask for myself, but for the sake of my lady, I must. She's to the manor born and risks her friends' disapproval by marrying me. Your approval would eliminate that embarrassment."

"And elevate you," Lord Santos retorted.

Michael shrugged. "That's incidental, my lord. Anything less than your full approval wouldn't be just to my lady."

Lord Santos didn't answer. Why did the man make him push so hard? Michael hadn't expected any resistance. A marriage without Lord Santos's full approval wouldn't provide him the widespread support he needed among the icers. And giving his niece anything less would also provoke ridicule in Cradle City and among his Consortium fellows at a time when their acceptance and approval of him was valuable.

"I could invoke a right to blood-debt," Michael added hesitantly. "I did save her life. I believe Ballendian law would uphold me in my claim."

"Ha! So that's your reason for not invoking it to begin with. All those lies about duty," Lord Santos said angrily. "I'll not let you invoke it now. I won't have it be said that I sold my own kin to pay a blood-debt. You have my approval for the marriage."

"Thank you, sire," Michael said, relieved.

"I ask only one thing in return."

Michael felt a twinge of fear, realizing now that Lord

Santos had forced Michael to drive a hard bargain to leave room for uncontested acceptance of some terms of his own.

"Allow me to set the date of the ceremony," Lord Santos asked wearily.

Was that all? Michael looked at him suspiciously. "I have only a few days leave left," he said.

"When will your next leave be?"

"Not for a year," Michael said. "Are you asking us to wait that long?" Could just an engagement of his niece to a iceman serve Lord Santos equally well in the elections? An engagement that could be broken before the year was done? Michael felt panic welling up inside. A year-long engagement would be as bad as no engagement at all.

"I cannot make arrangements for a festive wedding of the magnitude befitting Lady Jacinta's station in just a few days," Lord Santos said. "But you won't have to wait a year. I can arrange a special leave for you. I won't take any more time than necessary for proper arrangements." He gave the impression of a man accepting the inevitable who also was determined to make as agreeable as possible an unsatisfactory turn of events.

"*Ship Lisbon* is scheduled for departure in less than a week," Michael reminded him.

"I'll arrange a transfer from *Ship Lisbon*," Lord Santos said. "The Corps generally accommodates sponsors of my rank."

"Yes, sire, of course," Michael said, breathing a little easier now. "I'll leave the date to you and to my Lady Jacinta."

There it was. A simple assurance that Michael and Jacinta wouldn't marry hastily, which would have served Michael just as easily, but not the candidate for the Earth's ambassador seat. A resplendent ceremony and an unforgettable celebration in Cradle City that would filter down to the meanest of icer servants; indeed, it would employ hundreds extra at a generous wage and would send home gifts of surplus food to icer families. Perhaps there would even

be a holiday called at Consortium-controlled operations in
Cradle City and in the melts out on the ice. No doubt Lord
Santos was prepared to make the most of a serendipitous
combination of a wedding and an election, all favorable
for persuading voters in the District to think kindly of Lord
Santos.

Lord Santos smiled for the first time. "Send Lady Jacinta
to me. I'll discuss the plans with her," he said, signifying
Michael's dismissal.

She was waiting for him on the balcony, a wordless query
in her eyes. Michael smiled and nodded. "He wants you to
come to his study to discuss wedding plans." He thought
she would be pleased. Instead, she frowned.

"Just, 'send her to me and I'll tell her the plans,' " she
said unhappily. "Not a word about consulting me as to
whether I really care to marry you or not."

"If you had expected that much consideration from him,
you wouldn't have needed to marry me to escape from
him."

He saw her shiver, though with the morning sun halfway
to its zenith and the whole balcony bathed in sunlight, she
couldn't be cold.

"Well, I suppose I should go," she said. "I'm probably
supposed to be excited about his wanting a big wedding
for me."

"Yes, I believe that's what's expected."

"It's probably also expected that I'd want to select a
wedding gown," she said. "Would you like to go to the
Cradle emporiums with me tomorrow? I could be done
quickly, and then we could slip away, like we did the other
day when we took Anselem to the Port Authority."

She actually looked eager, and Michael was tempted. But
he shook his head. "I can't."

"Can't? What else could you possibly have to do?"

Michael sighed indulgently. "No doubt he'll have the
banns posted this Sunday, so I'd like to go to see some
friends before then, icer friends."

"Oh," she said, sounding disappointed.

"It wouldn't be very fitting in the future."

"Probably not, though I don't know that I'd worry about what was proper and what was not. I mean, Lord Santos's approval not withstanding, this marriage will be a shock to the starborn." She laughed brittlely.

"Well, since it would surely be improper, would you like to come with me?"

"To City Under?" she asked, amazed at first and then with impish delight. "Why not? It could be interesting."

CHAPTER
9

They left the gyro at the end of the dirt road that was really nothing more than ruts that narrowed into an alley lined with open-air stalls. It was barely dawn, and frost brought by a fresh cold off the glaciers glistened from the reflected light of fires that burned in big clay pots. The pots belched inky smoke that mingled unpleasantly with the stench that rose from the gutters, which Jacinta was beginning to suspect were nothing more than open sewers. She brought a fold of her cloak over her nose and mouth to lessen the assault on her senses, thought she'd gain some relief with her own perfume. The smell penetrated, and she almost retched.

At least she'd had sense enough to wear sturdy shoes, and the plain, gray cloak protected her from the mud splatters and grit. Michael had nodded his approval and only requested that she remove the glittering lenses from her eyes. She had complied, not quite understanding his reason for making the request.

She walked behind him, trying to follow his even footsteps. It was impossible to walk side by side in the teeming market, and she gratefully gave him her place in front by rank and status so he could make a path. But even following was difficult; the ground was uneven and the crowds pushy.

Even at this hour the icers were hawking and bargaining for the wares set out in baskets or hampers. She shrank with disgust at the sight of uncovered food, set in crates above the sewage in the gutters. The people were ugly, tall and gaunt, and with shriveled or pock-marked skin, their foreheads nearly touching as they bent over the baskets. She could hear their complaints about the goods, and the sharp replies from the owners. Every hamper was thronged by bent people, manned by bent people in smocks or aprons, and always there was a child nearby who wore a dress that was too thin or whose hands were blue with cold. With each step, Jacinta regretted her decision to come and longed to ask Michael to take her back. Only a morbid curiosity kept her following his easy pace.

There was no color here, save for some of the fruits and vegetables that must have been grown in greenhouses. The icers were monotonous in their thick, brown shawls and tattered, black aprons. She noticed the vacant stares they drew from some of the shopkeepers as well as the angry looks; Michael's Corps uniform was the only one in the marketplace, and as plain as her cloak was, it was unique in that it was unpatched, clean, and not coarse.

They were not really *in* City Under, she realized, just on the southern fringe, where the slanted rays of the morning sun penetrated the shadow cast by Cradle City. She was surprised to hear birds chirping and chattering; they always darted off the balcony so quickly when she tried to get a closer look. She still couldn't see them, but she heard them distinctly. Water dripped from the ceiling, whether from condensation or seepage she did not know, but it was sufficient to make sticky pools of mud that were completely unavoidable. Her shoes and the bottom of her cloak were covered with what she hoped was only mud.

Finally, Michael stopped at a fruit stall, which even to Jacinta's unaccustomed eyes was a step above the portable hampers and looked better kept than most of the shacks they'd passed. It was well stocked with unbruised produce, and attended by a crone who wore a thick, green shawl and a man's cap.

Michael picked up an orange. "May I have this one, Old Mother?" he asked, tossing it jauntily in the air.

The woman snatched it from midair, snarling loudly. It took Jacinta a moment to realize the woman had said, "Only if y've coin t' pay." Then the scowling slits of eyes grew wide with amazement. "Mikey boy," she gasped. "I thought we'd seen th' last of y' when the sticks took y' 'way. Then 'twas true. Y'r in th' Corps of Means and n' th' gaol fer y' evil pranks!"

"Shh," he warned, "or they might take you yet for putting me up to them!"

The old woman cackled with good humor. "Look at y' now, fat as a starborn lord and j'st as handsome. Y'even soun' like a starborn. Does m' ol' eyes good j'z' t' look at y'. Do th' treat y' well as y' look?" she asked, suddenly concerned.

"Once off Earth, most starborn don't even know what an icer herald means," he replied.

She smiled, showing yellow, broken teeth. "But y' 'aven't come t' see th' likes of me. Y'd not care tha' I've worried about y' all these years. Tiz Hansen y' want, so get on wi' y'. 'E's inside stuffin' 'is breakfast, th' lazy, ol' glutton!" Her chiding stopped when she realized Jacinta was with Michael, standing silently behind him. The old eyes searched for a clue to identity, but Jacinta had discreetly kept her hand under the folds of her cloak.

"Thank you, Old Mother," Michael said as he brushed past her hamper, towing Jacinta by the hand.

"Is she your mother?" Jacinta asked.

"No. What makes you ask that?" Michael asked with genuine surprise.

"You called her 'Old Mother.' "

"A respectful form of address among icers," he said, leading her up a short staircase and pushing through a timber door that lead into a dimly lit room.

A grease-paper window provided some light, a cooking charcoal burner in a stone fireplace took the chill out of the air. The floor was rough-hewn timber, two stools and a table the only furnishings. A paper picture from a packing box was tacked on the wall, its edges curled and brown.

A man, gray-haired but younger than the woman outside, sat at the bench, mopping something greasy from a cracked plate with a crust of bread. His eyes darted up at Michael, and Jacinta thought she saw a flash of surprise before his face became expressionless again. He pushed his chair back and hesitantly wiped his mouth on his sleeve.

"Tiz 'bout time y'v come," he said quietly. "Or should I speak like the starborn do? Perhaps you've forgotten the icer tongue as easily as you forgot your people."

"You knew I would come," Michael said.

"Did I?" He shrugged. "Some say you could have come a week ago."

"Plans change, sometimes for the better."

He grunted and nodded. "And what's this?" He pointed a bony finger at Jacinta.

"My bride to be, the Lady Jacinta."

The man's eyes didn't show amazement or even horror, either of which Jacinta would have expected. Instead, she thought she detected a touch of amusement.

Michael, however, didn't reciprocate with good humor. "I've brought her here so that you'll know who she is," he said. He turned and slipped Jacinta's hood down so that her head was bare. "Take a good look at her. I want you to be able to recognize her face, Hansen," he continued, "and to honor her well-being."

Hansen's eyes narrowed and hardened. "Do you know what you're doing?" he said angrily. "This is crazy."

In two steps Michael crossed the room and grabbed the scrawny shoulders. "You owe me," Michael said.

"And you'd collect it like this?" Hansen said, no mistaking the loathing and disappointment.

"I demand it," Michael said.

For a moment, a very tense moment, Jacinta watched

them hold each other's cold stares. She was bewildered and frightened by the exchange. Then the older man conceded.

"So be it," Hansen said.

Michael released his shoulders, and Hansen sagged back onto the stool. He glanced at Jacinta, suddenly looking sheepish.

"Welcome, my lady," he said, and rose stiffly from the stool to make a short bow. "I have few comforts to offer that befit your station, but what I have is yours."

Jacinta flushed and nodded slightly to acknowledge his sudden politeness. She had not expected to be well received by icers, nor had she expected Michael to force due respect from one.

"You speak perfect English," she said, both because it had surprised her and because she was at a loss for anything truly appropriate to say, considering what had just transpired.

"It's a lie that we're untrainable," he said, smiling as if teasing, but Jacinta took it as a declaration, too.

"Surely you know that I'm already convinced," she said.

"I pray that's true," Hansen said.

"Sit down, Jacinta," Michael said. "If I know Hansen, he's lying about not being able to offer comforts. Perhaps the stool is crude, but the cool ale he keeps is as fine as any on Earth. And better than the foul brew they serve on *Ship Lisbon*." Michael was smiling again, the confrontation with Hansen seemingly forgotten. His manner as he led her to the shaky stool was one of camaraderie, and unmistakably, Hansen displayed it now, too.

Hansen tilted his head back and bellowed, "Maria! Bring us ale. And be sure the glasses are clean!"

"Maria is here?" Michael asked, taking the other stool for himself.

"Where did you think she'd be?" Hansen asked as he reached under the table to pull out a crate. He sat down on it.

"After three years?" He shrugged. "I'd have thought she'd have married."

"Not too many icers as, um, *liberal* as the Jivar men," Hansen said, with a glance at Jacinta. "But I keep her around. She's a lazy thing, but a far sight prettier to watch than the old woman."

From a door in the back of the shack that Jacinta had not noticed, a girl entered. She had dark, shiny hair, a complexion far more pale than most icers, who tended to be sun-browned or at least olive-skinned, like Michael. Jacinta noticed her start of recognition when she saw Michael. Maria recovered quickly and brought a brimming pitcher of pink ale and a tray of frosty glasses to the table. Michael, Jacinta noticed, gave the girl a broad smile, which she returned warily.

"There'd better not be muck in the bottom, or I'll thrash you to an inch of your life," Hansen warned as the girl set the glasses before them.

"They're clean, Hansen," Maria replied tartly, and she poured the ale.

Jacinta couldn't help but notice that there was no herald on Maria's hand. When she placed the glass before Jacinta, she grasped the girl's hand and rubbed the place where the herald should be. There was no makeup or dirt to rub off; Maria's wrist was not tattooed. "Are you a fringe worlder?" Jacinta asked.

"No starborn would be living among icers, my lady," she girl replied softly, withdrawing her hand.

"Fringe worlder. Ha! That's funny." Hansen laughed raucously. "She's a . . ." His voice trailed off and his humor waned.

"I'm a foundling, my lady," the girl said, quietly withdrawing.

Jacinta looked first at Hansen and then at Michael, hoping for a clue as to why even a foundling wouldn't have a herald.

"She means she's a bastard," Michael told her grimly. "The result of a union between a starborn and an icewoman."

"She should still have a herald," Jacinta said, then reconsidered. "Oh, I see. Her mother deliberately didn't bring her in for coding because that would have revealed who the father was, which in turn would have created a scandal."

"For the starborn man, it would have been a scandal. But for the icewoman, such a child is a death warrant," Hansen said.

Jacinta shook her head. "It's a crime for some starborn, Ballendian women, for example, to have children out of wedlock. But it's not a crime that's punishable by death."

"It is if you're an icewoman. The child has starborn genes, and those are not to be mixed with our genes, which some believe are not as fine as yours," Hansen said, taking a swig of the ale.

"Still, they're not killed," Jacinta said, stubbornly.

Hansen shrugged. "They come in the night to take them away. No one ever sees them again."

Jacinta shook her head, not believing.

"Maria's one of the few who reached maturity. Michael's father took the mother in when her own family wouldn't keep her," Hansen explained.

"They were ashamed," Jacinta said. "Ballendians feel similarly about children born out of wedlock."

"Shame has nothing to do with it," Michael said. "The starborns' bastards can't be registered in Cradle City by the responsible man, and since such unions are forbidden, the woman can't claim it's an iceman's child, at least not any longer than it takes for them to run the chromosome tests they do before the tatoo. So the best the woman could hope for was to have an understanding husband who would help her keep the child concealed. But a hidden child means an extra mouth to feed, and sooner or later comes a poor harvest or hard times, and the child is turned out in the streets."

"That's cruel," Jacinta said.

Michael shrugged. "Icers view them as another burden placed on them by the starborn, but it's one they can turn their backs on, and most do. If the child is female, it may survive."

"The prostitutes?"

Michael nodded.

"But some are cared for by their families, like Maria."

"Yes."

"What happens if she's caught?"

"You tell me what the penalty is if you have neither a herald nor the more subtle identity chip planted under your skin somewhere."

"Nonregistration is treason. Unauthorized aliens face any variety of penalties, from deportation to death."

Michael nodded and refilled his glass. Hansen, she knew, was watching her closely for some sign of remorse. It was true that she had never heard of starborn bastards before, but if their fate was unjust, there was little she could do about it. She, too, was without help or protection, a pawn, a nothing, even if better treated.

Hansen scowled silently, and might have said something more about the bastards' plight, but the moment was interrupted by loud voices outside the fruit stall. The old woman's voice could be heard above others, furiously protesting even as the door burst open. A shabby iceman burst inside, with the old woman close behind.

"I tol' 'em y' ha' guests, Hansen, but th' filthy scum wouldn't wait!"

"I h' t' see y' now," the man pleaded. "Th's n' food, n' cheese, n't'ng."

"Yuh lazy good-for-n't'n," the crone shouted.

"Let 'm be, woman, and close the door," Hansen ordered softly.

The crone cast a contemptuous glance at the newcomer, then backed out the door.

"What is it, Martin?" Hansen said.

The man's hair was long and greasy. A coat too long for him fell open, revealing a shirtless chest of protruding bones. Below the waist he wore a filthy sarong belted by a rope. He pulled the cap off his head, his eyes darting from the well-dressed visitors to Hansen. He fidgeted nervously, uncertain of what to do now that he'd gained entrance.

"If you braved the old woman's scathing tongue and dodged her broom to get in here, yuh must have something important to say."

"Th' woman's been turned away from 'er job in Cradle. We need food, j'st t' tide us o' 'til she fin's another job," he said.

"Face it, Martin, your woman's too old for another job in Cradle," Hansen said gently. "They don't want to look at any but healthy young icers. You'll be lucky if they take you in the melts."

Martin fingered the hat. "We're not so ol'," he said bitterly. "We can work hard."

"They never did like your looks; too many pockmarks, and too skinny," Hansen said with a shrug. "I'll give y' the food to last out the week, then you go see Tom. He'll put y' to work when y' tell 'im I sent y'."

"Th' only way?" It was a plea, not a question.

Hansen nodded. "I kept her in Cradle as long as I could. But with her looks gone and the cough, I can't place her again. When that girl-child of yers buds, send her around to see me. If she's healthy enough, there's always kitchen work for comely girls. But for now, be grateful for the melts," he chided. "Now, we'll get y' the food. Maria!" he shouted, but the girl had already slipped into the room, her arms burdened with a hefty load bundled in a flour sack. Hansen sighed when he saw her. "I know, y' saw them come in. Well, give it to him. Then hurry and bring the special ale for our guests, the stuff in the blue bottle."

Martin left wordlessly, and Maria scurried back through the other door.

"You're a generous man," Jacinta ventured to say.

Michael choked on a laugh and sputtered ale.

"Now that's not nice," Hansen admonished Michael sternly.

"You just bought a tenement full of votes for Master Rayks, and the Lady Jacinta thinks you're a generous man," Michael said, shaking his head.

"Master Rayks?" she said. "The Constantinian who runs surface transportation?"

Michael turned to Jacinta. "Hansen is Master Rayks's servitor. He distributes certain Consortium goods in such a way that each pound of grain and every crock of cheese assures hundreds of icer votes. Our friend Martin will go back to his family with food from Hansen, and in minutes word will have spread to everyone he knows: Master Rayks doesn't let an icer down when the going is tough. Feed five people for a week on food their own labor has paid for ten times over, and it will buy the vote of every friend Martin has. Maybe a hundred or even a thousand. Each of them thinking that when his own woman is too old to work in Cradle or his joints too rotted, too stiff even to work in the melts out on the ice, Master Rayks's man Hansen will bail him out."

"And Hansen sells the best of the food in the stall out in front," Jacinta guessed.

"You catch on faster than I thought you would."

"But a man has to make a living, and Hansen is your friend."

"Yes," Michael said moodily.

Maria was back with another pitcher.

"The special ale for your lady?" Hansen asked.

Michael nodded and downed the last of the pink brew.

"I hope you find this to your liking, my lady. I've kept this ale for a special guest, such as yourself." Hansen poured sparkling, gold liquid into her glass. "Taste it. See if you don't agree that it's fine. An off-world brew, highly prized even on its planet of origin."

Jacinta raised the glass and sipped expectantly. The ale went down smoothly, pleasantly, so she swallowed more as Hansen poured for Michael and himself. She was suddenly aware that the air was almost intoxicating with the pungent odor of apples. She looked at the crate Hansen was sitting on, trying to puzzle out why it would be marked "oranges from Galilee" when she smelled apples so strongly. She heard Hansen talking again.

"Stay a moment, Maria. Your brother will want to know how it goes with you," he was saying.

"My brother? Oh, Mikey," Maria said.

And if she didn't think of Michael as her brother, Jacinta couldn't help wondering just what was he to the pretty, dark-haired woman?

"Not too tart, I hope, my lady. Just enough to be thirst-quenching?" Hansen said.

Jacinta nodded and took a few more swallows. Maria must have put more coals in the fire; she felt warm, and very thirsty. She drank more of the ale, and felt a gush of refreshing coolness.

"Not too strong?" Hansen said.

Jacinta shook her head, but the room still swayed when she thought she had stopped. The smell of apples was overpowering. She blinked to fight a growing vertigo.

"It is too strong," she heard someone far away say. "She should lay down."

Yes, she agreed, but where? In this filthy dwelling, where can Lady Jacinta rest her head? But they found her a place when she was well past caring about the dirt.

Michael cradled Jacinta in his arms until he felt her completely relax and she closed her eyes, then he pulled his arms out from under her and arranged her cloak as a cover. "I hope the dose in that bottle wasn't meant for icers," Michael said nervously. "The starborn are so little; she wouldn't need as much."

"It's a child's dose," Maria said as she slipped a wooden bar over the door. "She should have nothing worse than a few minutes of headache when she awakens."

"What have you done, Mikey boy?" Hansen said quietly. "Fallen in love with a starborn woman?"

Michael took one last look at Jacinta. She was breathing evenly, looked peaceful. He got up from his knees and took the stool opposite Hansen, rested his hands on the tableboards and laced his fingers.

"I've done what I set out to do," Michael said quietly.

"I've done it well, and now I've come back."

"Are you? Are you the same Mikey who went away?"

"The very same," Michael said, "and I resent your even questioning it."

Hansen gave a long, baleful stare. "What would you do if you were me? I knew you'd survived a shuttle crash, that you were picked up by rescuers, and last seen in the company of a Corps of Means event investigator. What kind of events do you think those sticks investigate between shuttle crashes? Do you have any idea of how many patriots are dead because of them? But here you are, not only alive, but with a starborn woman you say will be your bride. And if you were me, you'd be wondering the same things I'm wondering."

"You didn't know I was in Castle Santos?" And when Hansen shook his head, Michael shrugged. "I thought surely some of the servants were patriots and would get word to you."

Hansen scowled. "I had one in there. She was diddling one of Santos's own sons until not long ago."

"Just one patriot among a hundred servants?" Michael asked, unable to hide his surprise.

"It's almost impossible to get patriots into Cradle City these days, especially into Castle Santos. Even people with spotless profiles are turned away if they so much as have a wife's cousin who's a known patriot."

"It sounds like you've made them more nervous than they care to let on," Michael said with approval. "The official reports I've read make it sound like the terrorists are nothing that normal Consortium security precautions can't handle. They also emphasize the double-X chromosomes they have found in terrorists. I got worried enough about that one to look into it pretty thoroughly, wondered if maybe I had an extra X chromosome, too, and might be accused of being a terrorist."

"Did you?"

Michael shook his head. "And if you look carefully at the reports, you eventually figure out the source is the same, one guy. Probably still running tests on the poor slob."

"He's dead by now," Hansen said flatly. "They don't even pretend to give icers justice anymore. But we've changed the way we work, too. Small cells of patriots who have only one contact. No one knows who anyone else is, so that even drugs don't help much when they do catch anyone." Hansen leaned forward. "We also have off-world support now. Highly placed off-world support."

"I guessed as much when my shuttle crashed," Michael said, uneasily. Off-world support had to mean Star Treaty World support, worlds not aligned with the Council of Worlds, though technically not at war with them, either. The fringe worlds had had a separate alliance, too, but after the wars, fringe held no more significance than approximate coordinates. "You had someone besides me on *Ship Lisbon*, didn't you?"

Hansen shrugged noncommittally.

"When we left the Dolphinian orbit, I started getting anonymous messages on my vid. I didn't even know that was possible, especially on a ship that always had navigators plugged into the brainjars. I finally figured out that it had to be one of the navigators. We took on four at Dolphinia, but I couldn't figure out which one it was."

"If it was a navigator, you didn't need to know which one. All you needed to know was that you had to be on the little shuttle when it left *Ship Lisbon* for Earth, and then to be prepared to save Jacinta Renya's life so that Lord Santos would be indebted to you, which apparently worked quite well."

"The messages didn't say anything about killing two of our own people," Michael said, watching Hansen carefully for his reaction.

"They were no good to themselves or anyone else," Hansen said, too easily for Michael's satisfaction.

"What the hell is going on? We kill icers now, too, and don't care?"

"We care," Hansen said, "but we do it anyhow. We minimize where we can, and we use scum, like those poachers, when it suits us, so that better people aren't expended needlessly."

"Better people?" Michael said, his eyebrows raised in surprise. "I'd expect to hear that from a starborn, but not from an iceman. The whole idea is to make them accept us as equals, or have you suddenly begun believing that genetic manipulation does make better people?"

"I only meant there are greedy bastards in every gene-pool," Hansen said, "and a few less in exchange for knowing you still were committed to . . ."

"A test?" Michael said, feeling struck. "I spent three years in the Corps of Means to prepare for this mission, and you had to test my commitment by putting me in a kill-or-be-killed position with a couple of icers?"

"You may have been the first iceman to join the Corps of Means, but you were not the last. It turns out that it improves the Consortium's image with the Council of Worlds. Some of the other icers who became Corpsmen seem to have forgotten their origins," Hansen said coldly. "I'm not going to apologize for it, Mikey. We had to know."

But Michael shook his head. "They didn't know who I was. I tried to talk to one of them when I took him to the shuttle. He'd never heard of you. All he wanted was the gold, of which there wasn't any. I might have been killed myself before I figured out either these weren't the right guys or they'd turned on you. It didn't occur to me that you'd set them up."

Hansen frowned. "We sent them to take the gold for our cause. We'd never have seen them again if they had gotten any."

"You don't know that for sure," Michael said.

"They bragged to their friends that they'd be rich when they came back out of the tundra, rich with starfarer gold."

"But what about me? They might have killed me."

"Even with their guns, we knew they were no match for you. And we had to know if you were still with us. I still had my doubts when you didn't report as ordered."

"I came as soon as I could," Michael said, still not satisfied.

"But not until you'd managed a little tryst with the starborn lady," Hansen said.

Michael glanced down at Jacinta. Maria had put her shawl under Jacinta's head and was sitting next to her, knowing, Michael thought, that he would be comforted by her keeping watch.

"She won't sleep very long," Maria said softly.

Hansen grunted. "It's her way of telling us we're wasting time. We've more important things to discuss now that we know you're committed. Things have changed since you've been gone. The stakes are higher. We must not only destroy Castle Santos, but discredit the Consortium as well. If we fail, Earth will have lost all hope of self-rule."

Michael sighed and nodded. "The ambassadorial election," he said. "I've kept abreast as best I could through just reading one-sided starfarer reports about the Consortium and Earth. An ambassador seated on the Council of Worlds could open trade with Earth, instead of its just being an outpost world."

"Some people think some good could come of it," Hansen said quietly.

But Michael shook his head. "Not as long as there's the antiquities as the only resource, and not while those are controlled by the Consortium."

"Technically, they're not controlled by the Consortium," Hansen said.

"The means to get at them are," Michael said. "Icers don't have thermal drills and drop shafts and lift shafts, or even transportation to take them off the ice." He paused and looked up at Hansen. "Is this another test, Hansen? To see if three years in the Corps of Means has changed my point of view?" When Hansen didn't answer, Michael leaned back on the stool. "If I didn't care what happened to Earth, I would have transferred before *Ship Lisbon* returned to Earth. You'd never have heard from me again."

Hansen just nodded. "We had to be sure," he said simply.

"Destroying Castle Santos won't be easy."

Michael allowed himself a small smile. "Sure it will. I'm going to do it single-handedly. I've even planned when and how."

Hansen did not look as pleased as Michael expected him to.

"I'll listen to your plan, Mikey," Hansen said, "and if it's a good one, I'll present it to the other master planners."

"Master planners. You have some kind of hierarchy now?" And when Hansen nodded, Michael asked, "Who are they?"

"I told you about the cells. I'm your contact. For now, you're a cell of one. That's all you need to know."

Michael frowned. "When this started, we were all people who could trust each other because we'd known each other all our lives. I don't think I like this cell stuff."

"It's not a matter of your liking or not liking. It's just the way it is," Hansen said. "You have to understand that we haven't been idle for three years. Our organization is far more effective than your father or I ever dreamed it could be. The Consortium doesn't admit it in public, but we're a force to be reckoned with."

Michael considered for a moment, then nodded. "All right then, listen up. I'll do it on my wedding day. Ramon Santos and his son Cosimo will be hosting the wedding reception. Your job will be to be in a zepp-craft at Castle Santos when Jacinta is put on board for the bride chase. This is how it will work," he said.

Michael was aware that Hansen was frowning as he explained the details, but his questions were well considered and even helpful to Michael in thinking though parts of the plan that weren't as well worked out as he'd originally thought. Its success, from Michael's viewpoint, depended a great deal on Hansen being able to slip into the traffic pattern so as to be able to take Jacinta away to safety. That, however, seemed not to be a problem to Hansen.

"I may be able to get one of Lord Santos's own zepp-craft out of the Consortium repair bay, and the livery's no problem at all," he said. "But even if we found a way to keep all the servants at home that day, they'd be more likely to cancel the wedding than to fill in with guards from the Consortium. That part of your plan must be changed."

"I can't bring down a castle of plasteel and stone over a hundred of our people," Michael said. "You can't tell me they're greedy bastards. Even if they're not patriots, they're just trying to feed their families. You can't expect me to let them go with the starfarers."

Hansen didn't answer.

"Hansen," Michael said warningly. "I won't do it."

"Sometimes for the greater good . . ."

"No!"

"Sometimes civilians . . ."

"No!" he repeated.

Hansen sighed and thought for a while, then shook his head. "I don't know how we can keep them safe without arousing suspicion."

"They'll all go to watch the chase from the balconies," Maria said softly.

Hansen and Michael looked at her. She was still sitting next to Jacinta, her hands folded quietly in her lap.

"You said the kettles power the support structure for the castle," she said. "Can you leave the balconies standing?"

"Of all the stupid . . ." Hansen started to say.

"Not the balconies, but perhaps the tarmac where they keep all the vehicles. It's big enough to have its own feed from the kettles," Michael said, improvising quickly.

Maria smiled. "You could tell them yourself, Mikey," she said, "that you want them to watch from the tarmac. Promise them a merry chase. It's good luck to cheer the bridegroom during the chase. They'll do as you ask."

Michael smiled back and then looked at Hansen. He was nodding. "It would require your personal invitation, and one Lord Santos wouldn't countermand."

"I can do that," Michael said. "And I'll make sure Lord Santos's guests know the best place to watch the chase is from the balconies and the parapets. The worst part is going to be making sure Lord Santos and Cosimo are inside when it happens."

"But not her," Hansen said, gesturing to Jacinta's prone form.

"But not Jacinta."

Hansen shook his head. "She's one of them."

"She comes out," Michael said. "That point's not negotiable."

Hansen glanced at Maria, who was staring at Jacinta. He shrugged and nodded. "So be it, if the master planners all agree."

"And how will I know if I have their agreement?"

"Come back tomorrow night."

Michael shook his head. "Tell them it's this or nothing. I don't need their agreement. I only need you to be there with that zepp-craft. You give me your word here and now, your personal word."

Hansen sat there so long without speaking that Michael thought he was going to refuse. "You're putting both our lives in that woman's hands. She's not even a sympathizer, just a spoilt starborn who is dissatisfied with her lot in life. If she doesn't hold her tongue, we'll both be dead before the sun goes down."

"I told you that she can't go back to the Corps of Means unless she marries me."

"Considering what you're about to do, I think I'd rather hear that she was blindly in love with you."

So would I, Michael thought. For a fleeting moment, he imagined what it would feel like to hear her say that she loved him and know that she meant it. What might he be tempted to do then? He didn't dare consider it. He shook his head and looked at Hansen. Whatever it was that Hansen saw on his face made him smile sadly.

"You have my word, Mikey."

CHAPTER
10

There were voices, low and furtive. Strange sounds, thumps and dreams that wandered from the downy coverlet of her own bed to frightening, crawling things in an icer dwelling. Then the voices disappeared and the dreams shattered. There was a hard, uncomfortable feeling along her back and head. She was lying on something hard.

"Jacinta, are you all right?" she heard Michael ask.

Jacinta opened her eyes. Michael was leaning over her, his face filled with concern. "What happened?" she asked.

"You fainted," he said.

"I what?"

"Fainted," he said. "Do you feel better now?"

Hansen was behind him, his eyes wide with fear. "It was the ale," he moaned. "It was too strong, or bad perhaps. I should not have offered it. I will spill the rest in the gutter. The whole case. Oh, dear god, what will become of me when Master Rayks hears of this?"

"Hush, Hansen. She seems all right now," Michael said. "Are you, really? You gave me a scare, too."

"I think so," Jacinta said. She sat up and her head swam and throbbed.

"Drink this." Maria offered a cup of steaming broth. "It will dilute the ale."

With trembling hands, Jacinta gripped the cup and sipped the broth. It was scalding, but it settled the worst of the strange feelings, so she finished the brew.

When Maria handed her a second cup, she realized she was sitting on the floor by her stool. There were three empty glasses still on the table, but the pitcher of golden ale was gone.

Michael was on his knees next to her. "I'm sorry, Jacinta," he whispered. "I don't feel very well myself. The ale must have been bad, but I didn't have as much as you." He was drinking a mug of the broth, too. "We'll leave as soon as you're able."

"It's passing now," she said. "I'll be fine in a moment. But will you? My uncle will be scandalized if I have to drive the gyro."

"I can drive," he assured her.

"Help me up," she said. She felt absolutely stupid sitting on the floor with everyone watching her.

Effortlessly, he raised her up, steadying her until she smiled, signifying she was all right. If he had been ill at all, it had not affected him as it had her. She still felt weak in the knees.

Michael turned to Hansen. "We'll leave now."

Hansen danced nervously behind Michael and came out bowing to Jacinta. "I beg your forgiveness, my lady." And to Michael, furtively, he whispered, "Master Rayks will never forgive me if he hears of this."

The whining tone seemed out of character, but she nodded graciously. "He won't hear of it from me," she said. To Michael she added, "Let's go."

He opened the door and she hurried out. The crowd had thinned. None of the hawkers were left except those whose baskets had holes laced with twigs and fastened across and in which the poorest of produce lay, already rotting in the sun. With Michael following her, she quickly walked toward the alley where they had entered. She was eager to be away from the vacant stares and the disgusting stench that threatened to make her ill all over again.

In the alley, she walked even faster, until suddenly her way was obstructed by a sickly-looking boy no more than five years old, who stood with his hand outstretched, blue feet on the bare stones. She jerked back and started around him, only to find her way obstructed by a grotesque fence of children, none of them much taller than the baskets back in the market, blue hands outstretched like protrusions from skeletal shoulders set on balloon bellies.

Frightened, Jacinta stepped back and grabbed Michael's tunic. "What do they want? Why won't they let us pass?"

"They bar the alley when they see a starborn," Michael said softly. "He's sure to cast coins to them."

"Oh, god, their arms," she said. "No tattoos. They're bastards."

Grim-faced, Michael opened his coin purse and dumped it onto the ground. The children dived for the coins, fighting and scratching with an intensity such pitiful bodies should not have been able to sustain. The successful ones scurried off, disappearing through missing slats of packing plastic that fenced the alley.

"They're barely more than babes," Jacinta said indignantly.

"I know," he said, staring at the broken slat where the last one disappeared.

Realizing the futility of her wrath, Jacinta turned, blinking back insistently welling tears as she walked. She didn't feel in control again until they reached the gyro. But even at that, she didn't want to think of what she'd just seen, nor talk of it. She climbed into the passenger seat before Michael could aid her, and she stared out the viewplate.

As soon as Michael got in, he activated the thrusters and guided the gyro through the alleys, heading north along a track of rubble relatively free of vegetation, rapidly leaving City Under behind them. Hedgerows lining the track were greening, the tangles of growth dense and dark, then dwindling as the gyro sped onto the open tundra. Michael didn't stop the gyro until the glacier edge loomed before them. He sat staring up at it, the waters rushing through slush and mounds of white, melting ice, running past them into a virtual river of icy water.

"What did you think of it?" he asked, his voice almost as stony as she felt.

"What is this?" she said. "First, show Jacinta how the icers live, then take her to the glacier to show her just how ineffective the starborn are at changing it?"

"No," he said. "It was to remind me."

"You won't get far in the Corps with a chip on your shoulder," she said.

"I know," he said.

"Oh, great. Well, just remember that when I ask for my transfer off *Ship Lisbon*, and don't follow."

"I won't," he said. He opened the door and got out, picking his way over stones and debris, stopping about twenty feet away on a tiny hillock where the grass was greening.

She sat quietly, watching him stare up at the glacier. With the gyro powered down, she was getting chilly, but she didn't try to call him back. She supposed he was entitled to his reverie, or whatever it was that was going on between him and The Cold. Maybe some vow to stop it, though if the starborn couldn't, she knew an iceman couldn't either. He was a puzzle to her. She knew even before she'd seen how the icers lived in City Under that a kettle tender's life would be better, and she couldn't blame him for wanting that. But he had that before he'd ever met her. The question was why he would risk his future to help her, but then she supposed she knew. He'd gotten a taste of the starfarer's life, and he wanted to enjoy it to the fullest; and her uncle's sponsorship of him in the Corps of Means would expand possibilities. Maybe this was his last look at what he was leaving behind. He couldn't be regretting it, but she supposed he just might be feeling guilty. Maybe especially about the dark-haired girl.

At last he came back, and powered up the gyro. Hot air rushed in through the blowers. Michael turned the gyro around and drove slowly back the way they had come.

"Maria wasn't your sister, was she?" Jacinta asked without looking at him.

"Not really," he said.

"And her being a bastard, I suppose you . . . slept with her," she said. "Or was it your father who slept with her?"

Michael gave a choked laugh and looked away.

"You did, didn't you?" Jacinta said accusingly.

Michael shook his head. "Maria is my stepsister. We slept in the same bed from the time my father took her in. All of us. I was always in the middle because I was the littlest." Michael looked very strained and tired as he met her eyes. "Icers sleep together to keep warm."

"You expect me to believe that just because they're cold, icers don't do anything but sleep when they get in bed?"

"Not if it's a sister or even a stepsister they're sleeping with," Michael insisted.

"And you think she's just keeping warm when she goes to bed with Hansen?"

"I don't know," he admitted.

"But you wouldn't bother inquiring too closely, because Hansen is your friend, and you're grateful Hansen has taken her in."

"Something like that," he said.

"And you say icers are honorable folk," she said.

"If there's anything between Hansen and my stepsister, it doesn't matter whether I approve or not. They're both adults; they must live with their consciences, not mine."

"But what choice would she have if she didn't comply? He could just cast her out to live like those children. Or worse!"

"I don't think Hansen would do anything like that," Michael said tiredly.

"No, of course you wouldn't," she threw back.

"I've never done anything to you except help you when you needed it. So why do you look for ways to think poorly of me?"

"I'm not looking for anything. I'm just trying to understand," she protested.

"Then understand this. I am not like your uncle or your cousin. Hansen's not like them. If I thought he was forcing Maria, I'd kill him."

Jacinta swallowed hard. "I'm trying to understand. I want to trust you, but . . ."

"Yeah, sure. Hansen is, too. Everyone's trying to trust me, but no one's quite succeeding. Not you. Not Hansen."

"You mean that little scene when we came in. What was that all about?"

Michael shrugged. "Hansen is as much family as I have. I knew he wouldn't approve."

"And you wanted his blessings?"

Michael half-smiled. "Blessings would be asking too much, but I at least wanted him to accept you."

"I don't care if he accepts me or not," she said.

"No," he said slowly. "But I wish you'd learn that I do."

"I thought you only cared about your career in the Corps. I assumed that you wanted to get away from all this."

"You assumed wrong," he said.

"But you're leaving anyway, and now you're feeling guilty about it, is that it?" Suddenly she felt frightened. "Michael, are you going to back out of the wedding?"

"Is that all you can think of? Yourself? Hansen pandering for Rayks doesn't bother you. A woman like Maria doesn't disturb you. She wouldn't be worth your jealousy, would she?" He frowned darkly. "Dead boys stacked like logs did it, and the bastards. Jacinta, they are my people, and they live the way they do because of yours."

Jacinta shook her head. "I can't help them," she said, "and I don't think our marriage will do anything for their plight either."

"Neither do I," he said, "but I'd like to think that if you believed you could help them, you would."

"I would," she said.

"Would you?"

"Of course, but there isn't anything I can do for them. You know that."

"Maybe there is," he said.

"Like what?"

"Like being kind to them," he said. "To the servants, I mean. Let them want to speak well of you."

"So that they won't think ill of you for having married me?" she ventured. "So that this legend about you is perpetuated even when we're gone? Help you assuage your conscience?"

"Yes, but not how you mean," he said. "They haven't much happiness in their lives, but when they find out about our wedding, they'll be, well . . . first they'll probably be astonished, but they'll also be happy about it."

"Deliriously happy," she said.

"It would please me a great deal if you would add to that what you could," he said. "Arrange for your uncle to let them watch the bride chase from the tarmac."

"The bride chase?" she said.

He nodded. "They'll love the chase, especially when I win it."

"You natives are every bit as bawdy as Ballendians. Bride chases are a barbaric custom. Nothing more than symbolic rape."

"The whole thing is a sham, Jacinta. The wedding, the vows, all of it. What harm would it do for you to pretend to have a little compassion for my people and just make one day in their lives have a few minutes of fun?"

"All right," she said. "I'll have it arranged so that all the servants of Castle Santos can say they saw the legendary Michael Jivar catch the starborn lady."

His lips were pressed thin against his teeth. "You also need to invite them, each one, personally."

"I said I'd arrange . . ."

"They might not come if you don't ask them yourself," he said. "A personal invitation would mean more than an announcement."

With her own lips set firmly, she nodded.

"Is it going to be so difficult?" he asked, more angry, she thought, than really concerned.

Jacinta didn't answer him.

He stopped the gyro and turned to look at her. "Just once, I'd like to know what you really feel. I'd like to know without trying to guess."

She stared at him, the intensity in his eyes frightening her and undermining her strength. What would he think of her if she told him that nothing mattered except the wedding that would put her in control of her own life? How could he possibly understand that a Ballendian woman couldn't even have an ideology of her own? She wasn't fool enough to believe this excursion had not been at least in part for her benefit, and she had come away wiser. But so what? He kept looking at her expectantly.

"I will speak to every servant personally, and you can be sure that I will be both gracious and charming on your behalf."

"But how will you feel about doing it, Jacinta? How will you feel doing something I've asked of you? Does it please you to please me by helping my people have a bit of pleasure?"

"What the hell do you want from me?" she cried out. "I said I'd do it, didn't I?"

"Forgive my prying, my lady," Michael said glumly, and he accelerated the gyro to reckless speed.

Jacinta watched the tundra speed by, unable to admit even to herself what she was feeling.

The final morning of Michael's leave dawned cloudy and with the heavy kind of frost he remembered from the worst of his boyhood springs when tender plantlings perished in all but the hedgerows, where sturdier growth provided a bit of protection from the late snows. Even if it warmed enough to melt, the alleys became rivers of mud, and an unhealthy dampness invaded every dwelling until the dry, hot months of summer. And then what was left of the crops shriveled for lack of rain, even while the rivers swelled with meltwater from the glaciers. Few areas had adequate irrigation anymore; in the hottest summers just when crops were supposed to be growing, the meltwater came in torrents, first stripping irrigation canal definitions and then scouring the fields. Icers would move their shacks up into the rocks until the water subsided, usually unable to return to the basins until the cold returned. In years like this, few icers could live off the land, and were dependent on what they could earn from the starborn. They didn't care if Earth was represented in the Council of Worlds, or by whom, only that there was something to eat, and enough leftover for the children to eat, too.

Michael put his spare uniform in his duffle. It had been spotlessly cleaned and artfully mended to the most trifling detail by the palace staff. The rich civilian garb that had mysteriously appeared in his wardrobe in the first days of his leave, he left. He would need none of it.

Through the passglass, he saw Jacinta cross their balcony to the railing, pausing only to glance in his direction and to gesture for him to follow. Then she stared out at the sheet of ice that covered half the North American continent, ice that gleamed like a jewel in the morning sun. But for meals with her family, he had not seen her since the argument following the visit with Hansen. He felt badly about it, knowing that he had wanted something from her that she couldn't possibly give. He didn't know why he cared, for even if she could love him, even just a little, nothing could ever come of it. All it did was sadden him to think about all the futures that could never be.

Michael took a final look around the suite that had provided the richest comforts he'd ever known. Not for the first time, he wondered what someone like Jacinta had thought about while she was growing up in such splendor, and wondered if she would have wanted to trade it all for the more spartan life of a Corps of Means navigator if there had been any other way to escape her uncle. Michael had been to starfarer worlds and had seen with his own eyes that the starborn were not lying when they said that squalor the likes of Earth's didn't exist on theirs. He'd learned that the best

of the starborn couldn't even comprehend the meanness of
life on their planet of origin; there was nothing like it on
their worlds, not with their incredible ability to apply all
the technology they'd developed in two thousand years.
Cradle City's comforts, all but isolated by passlaws, kept
icers out of the starborns' lives. The best of them didn't
seem to understand a disparity even existed. The rest of
them who knew didn't care. No, that was too quick, too
easy. There was Jacinta, who knew but who was helpless
to do anything about it.

Michael closed the duffle bag, used the servants' comm
to ask that the duffle be delivered to the zepp-port, and then
went to follow Jacinta.

She was still staring out at the sparkling ice. Her long,
dark hair was simply parted, hanging in two strands bound
with rust ribbon that gave an illusion of braid. "I think
they've figured out I intend to keep the balcony clean of
eavesdropping devices, or perhaps my uncle just doesn't
care anymore. There's only the one optic working."

He nodded absently and took her hand. "Are you happy?"
he asked hoarsely. "Are you going to be happy?"

"I told you, Michael. They can only see us, not hear us.
You don't have to whisper sweet nothings."

"That wasn't play acting," he said. "I really want to know
if you're still happy about doing this."

"Of course I am," she said impatiently.

Michael hovered over Jacinta as she leaned back against
the railing. Being so close to her was almost intoxicating.

"They can't see us here," Jacinta said when he bent to
kiss her.

"Don't be so sure," he said, trying to ignore the sparkle of
silver lenses over her eyes. She was so hard to read with her
eyes covered this way. "I won't be back until the morning
of the wedding, and your uncle's spies will be expecting us
to kiss."

"Then we should move to the other side of the balcony
where we know it can have some useful effect," she said,
trying to push past him.

"No, don't . . ." he said. He straightened and stepped back. "I want to talk to you privately, I mean the real you."

She looked at him expectantly, and he could not resist touching her cheek. She did not shrink from him, and he put his hand behind her neck.

"You're going to be alone the next few weeks," he said. "They may not be easy times. Some people are bound to talk."

"Likely they won't do it in my hearing," she said. "Even if they did, do you think I would change my mind?"

"I hope not," he said sincerely. "But I . . ." He breathed and touched her lips with his own. This time she did not resist as he drew her against his chest and kissed her gently. "Have I done what's right for you? Will you want this when it's done?"

"Why are you worrying about that now?" she said, her forearms pressed against his chest to hold him away. "I've made my decision. Or is it yourself you're worrying about? Still feeling guilty for leaving your friends for a good career in the Corps."

"I've made my decision. We'll marry, but I wonder if you can get along without me afterward."

"Look," she said, obviously disturbed. "I admit I needed your help even to see there was a way to get back to the Corps and then to fool my uncle into believing it was all his idea. But I was on my own when I was in the Corps, and I did just fine. This time I won't have to worry about dealing with my uncle when my contract is over, because I won't ever have to come back to Earth again. I'll just have the Corps to deal with, and that I can do just fine on my own."

"Yes, but I just don't like thinking that you'll be alone again. I wish . . ." Michael closed his eyes and shook his head. He shouldn't wish.

Jacinta took a deep breath. "This fantasy we've created has become real to you, hasn't it?"

Unable to lie, he nodded.

"Now what?" she said. "Do we strike a new bargain? One that includes your bed, perhaps?" She shrugged, coldly, determinedly. "If that's what it takes."

"That's not what I want," he said, gruffly cutting her off. He released her from his hold but spoke close to her face. "I just wanted to know if you still want your galaxy of stars, now, while there's time. I have to be sure I'm doing the right thing for you. You'll have your stars, and you don't have to bargain from my bed for them. I promised that once, and I won't break my word."

"God save me from men who are determined to protect me," she said, laughing shakily.

Silently Michael took her hand. He felt only a little comforted; she had not changed her mind about wanting the stars, but he couldn't help knowing that for all her determination now, she might not be willing if she understood the real price she'd pay. In moments he'd have to leave, and when he returned for the wedding there'd be so little time with her. Roughly he pulled her into his arms and kissed her, feeling first her surprise and then such strong resistance that he let go of her with equal abruptness.

He thought she was going to slap him, and then when she didn't, he expected her to flee. She didn't do that, either. Instead, she reached for his hand and stepped into his arms, then kissed him, and for the first time he believed she wasn't just playing a role. He didn't know why she had chosen this moment; perhaps it was nothing more than pity or some kind of reward for sticking with the bargain. He didn't care about the reason. He just wanted to kiss her like this forever.

Lord Santos stared at the wall vid to watch the iceman kissing his niece. It had not disgusted him as he thought it might. It was in fact vaguely disappointing, too saccharine and terribly chaste. Of course, if he knew Jacinta, if that Neanderthal had tried to touch her breasts, she'd probably scratch his eyes out. He wondered what would happen on their wedding night. Would she submit to the big Corpsman? Or would he submit to her? God, that might be a scene worth watching.

"Brainroom, could we arrange a bridal nesting here at the castle?"

"If you mean for Lady Jacinta and Ensign Jivar, I cannot recommend changing the current plan for them to spend their wedding night in the Consortium Towers guest house. It was selected with great care. It is far enough from Castle Santos that the bride chase won't be over quickly, and the zepp-carriage we're using should be easily seen. The guest house faces west and is on Cradle City's highest tier, so it can be seen easily throughout the District. When the lights go out in the bridal couple's nest, the icers' celebration begins in earnest."

"The chase is a Ballendian custom," Lord Santos said. "What the icers want to see is the lights go out, right?"

"Yes."

"Well, they can see lights go on and off in Castle Santos just as well, perhaps even better. The clouds rarely come this low."

"Yes," the brainroom voice said. "While what you say is true, our data shows that even though it's not their custom, the bride chase appeals to the icers. Sales are very brisk on distance-vision enhancement devices, even simple ground-glass lenses. We assume they plan to watch the chase attentively."

Lord Santos nodded resignedly. By the simple act of posting the banns in the icers' churches as well as Cradle City, they'd created more favorable sentiment than he would have believed possible. The election observers arrived the day after the wedding, and the elections themselves would be the day after that. By nightfall, he would officially be the Ambassador from Earth.

"But if I understand why you might prefer to have the nesting here at Castle Santos, I might be able to arrange, well, shall we say, a closer view of what happens when the lights go out at the Consortium guest house?" the brainroom

voice said. "I can coordinate some additional security meas-
ures with the Consortium brainroom, which, of course, they
will put totally under my control for that night so that there
is absolutely no risk of recordings in Consortium brainjars
of such an intensely personal Ballendian event."

"You don't think you'd have any trouble justifying such
unusual arrangements?" Lord Santos asked.

"None, sire," the brainroom voice replied.

Lord Santos leaned back in his chair. This new household
monitor was gaining favor with him rapidly. He liked the
way it thought, especially the way it anticipated his needs.

"I also want you to arrange a companion for me," he
said.

"To be with you when the lights go out?" the brainroom
voice said. "Perhaps one who looks something like the Lady
Jacinta?"

Lord Santos smiled. "When the lights go out, it doesn't
matter what she looks like," he said.

CHAPTER
11

Maria watched Hansen as he stood at the door of the shack staring up at the white-hot sun. Nothing would stop him from sweating today, not if he were up to his neck in icy meltwater, which from the looks of the swells they all just might be in a week or two. But at least for today, no one would notice his sweating with such heat; they'd be too busy mopping their own brows.

Although it was late morning, the marketplace was crowded not with shoppers but with merrymakers. There wasn't an icer alive who didn't know that today Michael Jivar would wed the Lady Jacinta. No matter that Cradle City's starborn folk referred to Michael as the Corps of Means ensign and often alluded to his heroism in saving Lady Jacinta from certain death at the hands of knaves. The icers knew Michael wore their herald on his left wrist, and they marveled at his winning the hand of a starborn lady.

"They rejoice for him," Maria said as she watched a snake of dancers stream happily past the greasepaper window.

"Yes, and for things to come for themselves," Hansen said. "Dreams and nonsense."

"Is it so wrong to hope?" Maria wondered out loud.

"They dream of starborn for themselves tomorrow," Hansen said. "They'll not live to see their dreams come true."

"I know," Maria said wistfully. "No changes will come because of the wedding."

"Be grateful," Hansen said. He came back into the shack, shutting the door. He was wearing the gray and scarlet livery of Lord Santos. "You wouldn't like the changes that would come if Lord Santos were Earth's ambassador to the Council of Worlds."

Maria didn't answer. She didn't care who the ambassador was. Be it Lord Santos or Master Rayks, it wouldn't change her not having a herald to wear. Not that it bothered her all that much. Even if she had one, she'd only be able to work out on the ice, and she was pretty sure that stacking Hansen's goods and cooking for him was the easier life. She'd been grateful that he'd taken her in after the sticks captured Michael, and she had known that even if Michael returned, he could not stay. Still, she'd hoped against hope. She'd dreamed of a wife for him and a husband for herself, maybe even Hansen, though he had not actually wooed her. Then Michael really had returned, and the dream shattered. She'd known the second she saw Michael's face that he loved the starborn woman. She feared for her little brother as she had never feared for herself.

"The girl h' a good eye, Hansen," the crone said, looking him up and down. "'Ts perfect to th' smallest detail."

Maria shook her head. "Your hair's not right to play the part of imported talent. It'd be short like a Tridian or shaved in the style of Mathisons World."

"No, girl. They wear it like the starborn lords when they've been in service a while," Hansen corrected gently.

Maria reflected thoughtfully. "Then it should be trimmed and combed," she said, and pulled a razor from her apron pocket.

Hansen sat on a stool to let Maria trim the dark-dyed, freshly washed hair and smooth it to her liking with her fingers. "How do you always know these details?" he asked her. "You, who's rarely been in the streets, let alone near guards or the starborn."

Maria smiled. "The pictures on the tins and boxes," she said.

Hansen looked at her critically. "Why'd you tell me that?" he asked. "Why today, after all these years of me believing you were fey?"

Maria shrugged.

"You don't think I'm coming back today, do you?"

Maria stepped back and eyed her handiwork critically. "If you don't come back, it won't be because you've been betrayed by a false stitch in the clothes I've made for you. Nor by any weakness in your action. Michael won't fail either. If it's to fail, it will be her at the bottom of it."

"I'd like to think Michael wouldn't risk our lives for a starborn woman."

"Wouldn't he? Michael has always lived with danger; his father saw to that. Why would now be different?"

"That's why I've always liked him," Hansen said with a sudden grin, "and you should, too. You'd be dead if he hadn't met the sticks in the alley rather than let them into the shack where they'd find you."

"Yes, but there's the rub. Which life was worth more?" Maria asked. "Michael's or mine?"

"Michael's," Hansen said without hesitation.

Maria knew Hansen had never quite forgiven Michael for sacrificing himself for Maria without knowing for sure that the sticks had come because of the blood-debt or if they'd just come. And Hansen must be wondering now: If Michael could do that for a bastard stepsister like Maria, what would he do for the love of a starborn lady?

Taking his long, brown cloak from the peg by the door, Hansen wrapped it securely over the Santos livery.

"Do you have the paste to cover the herald?" Maria asked him.

He pulled a jar from his pocket to reassure her, and he smiled at her, something he rarely did. "Have my supper ready, girl. I'll be hungry when I return."

"I'll have it ready," she said softly, watching as he slipped out the door into the marketplace full of happy celebrators. If he didn't come back, she didn't know where she'd go.

In his room at Castle Santos, Michael changed into the fresh ensign's uniform that had been hanging in the wardrobe. It was the same rust and gray as the one he had discarded just before his bath, but the cloth was finer quality. Even the perfectly good Corps-issue boots had been replaced by sleek, black kane-hide ones, ground to a flawless sheen. Michael adjusted the decorative sword but replaced the gem-studded knife in the new uniform sheath with his own black-hilt stiletto. He took a slender coil of synthetic rope from his duffle and tucked it in his waistband, then smoothed the lapels of the uniform. Now he was ready.

He glanced at the wall vid. The big screen had been displaying event preparation status since he had awakened. According to the readout, Jacinta's zepp-speeder had just departed for the chapel, and his own craft was waiting in the tetheryard. He could hardly believe the time had actually come. He took a few deep breaths, then left the suite.

The family-wing corridor was filled with servants who were already cleaning Jacinta's chambers, scurrying with armloads of just-discarded clothes for the laundry and with fresh feathering for the bed. They would clean and freshen the entire wing with a great burst of energy so that the chambers would be finished before the wedding party returned, and then they would attend the guests who would throng the public rooms. Busy as they were, they all paused when they saw him.

"Congratulations."

"Happiness!"

"Kiss the bride for me!"

Icers all, lighthearted and happy to be cleaning up after him. Their joy only made him all the more nervous.

"You'll be out on the tarmac to watch the chase, won't you?" he asked them, each in turn.

"Wouldn't miss it," he heard, or comments like it, and some of the men even cuffed him on the arm, as they did to nervous grooms in City Under.

Outdoors, the heat was already oppressive, the feel of the air muggy. The sound of his kane-hide boots echoed smartly off the stone as he walked through the maze of terraces to the tetheryard with its dark, sprawling tarmac.

Cosimo was waiting for him. He wore a muscle-defining body suit the starborn favored, accented with a tasteful blazon of Santos colors. His dark, curly hair was as shiny as a crown. "I've been waiting for ten minutes," he said, glancing at his watch.

"I'm on time," Michael said crisply.

"They said you'd be early. I was supposed to keep you from seeing Jacinta. Some stupid native custom."

"They?" Michael asked.

"The advisers," Cosimo said.

"They should have realized that of all people, I'd know the custom. It's bad luck to see the bride in her gown until the wedding itself."

"Luck has nothing to do with it," Cosimo said. He pointed to a zepp-speeder halfway across the yard. Michael let him lead the way across the hot tarmac.

The chapel, an ancient military one, stood on a stone butte in the tundra. What had been a crumpled drill field six weeks ago had been repaved with what looked like ordinary cement to accommodate zepp-speeders and hovercraft. It was a tiny building when compared to the temple in Cradle City, but even though cordoned off so that only invited guests could get near, it was, Michael realized, far more suitable to Lord Santos's purpose. The chapel was one of the few relics still standing after two thousand years, lovingly maintained by a paramilitary religious sect until only forty years ago, then taken over by an off-world archaeological society, which still maintained it. The interior had been refurbished; Michael could still smell the newness of the posh red carpeting beneath his feet.

The chapel held only a few hundred people, all starborn in their finest garb, the muscle-definition suits for the young and trim, blousey chiffons for older folk and those whose bodies were anything less than perfect. They stared at Michael, who waited at the altar with a somber priest. Then Jacinta entered on her uncle's arm, and everyone turned to look at her. Not even Michael could tear his eyes away.

Jacinta was dressed in a white sari that was trimmed delicately with golden lace. Any other bride would have worn the colors of her bridegroom's herald, but the somber brown of the icers would be an affront. Tactfully, Jacinta had dipped into legends and had taken the ancients' color as her own. Rain pearls bound with the same golden thread in her tiara held her hair in place. Her navigation jacks were hidden by transparent pearls and gold leaf. Michael thought she looked more beautiful than ever before.

The ceremony, for all the pomp, was a disappointment. The red-robed priest chanted over the couple at the altar, then solemnly handed Michael a crystal cylinder containing Jacinta's papers—the record of her genetics, forebearers for six generations, the sum of which was stamped in the Santos herald with Jacinta's navigation star in the right corner. That was all to signify the tying of bonds for man and woman if they were starborn: no vows, as they did for icers, no ring or chain for either to wear. But those, Michael realized, would be meaningless in a Ballendian marriage, which was a formality for relocating chattel and documenting breeding lines. But for Jacinta, her nearly breathtaking beauty and the look of anticipation on her face, he would have been sorely disappointed in the mockery of this ceremony. Though it was through pearly lenses, she looked at him, not lowering her eyes. The Ballendian starborn were probably scandalized, but he was proud of her for defying custom before her family and peers.

When the brief ceremony was over, Jacinta took his arm, and they walked down a fresh red velvet runner to the outer door of the chapel, then under a tent of swords formed by a

Corps honor guard he hadn't even known would be there.

There were no well-wishers thronging the zepp-carriage, as there would be at the ox-cart in the icers' marketplace if this were a true icer marriage. The starborn bride had no true friends of her own; her uncle seemed to be accepting more congratulations than were offered to Michael or Jacinta. Later, in the castle there would be festivities, but none comparing to the wild celebrations among the icers.

Lord Santos and Cosimo rode in the zepp-carriage along with another honor guard, this one from the Consortium's security forces. The huge, open-topped carriage began moving toward the edge of the parade ground, floating out over the edge, then dropping almost imperceptibly. Michael took the crystal cylinder holding Jacinta's papers and secured it under his tunic. Jacinta squeezed his hand and flashed him a smile of triumph that her uncle could not see.

"I've never seen you look so happy," he whispered.

"Not as happy as I'll be when that crystal cylinder is in my hand," she whispered back. "God, I am so relieved. We did it, Michael. We did it!" Again Jacinta squeezed his hand. "Tomorrow I can negotiate my own contract with the Corps of Means. I can leave Earth and never return."

"What if your ship is sent to Earth orbit?" Michael said.

"I'll stay on board," she said. "He won't be able to force me to visit."

Michael did not have to ask who she meant.

At ground level again, the zepp-carriage wound its way over a freshly graded road that ran through one of the many icer valleys. For miles the road was lined with cheering icers who were pushing and shoving to get a glimpse of the couple. Michael heard the clear icer chant above the whine of the zepp's energy charger: "Long live Michael, long live Jacinta!"

"They're bold in addressing the Lady Jacinta that way," the honor guard captain said to Lord Santos.

"And you are remiss in yours," Michael said loudly enough to be heard this time. "She is now Madame Jivar."

The startled captain accepted the iceman's rebuke silently, but still looked for some sign from Lord Santos, as if he were eager to dispatch his troops into the throng to stop the chant.

"Let them be," Lord Santos said. "I haven't ever seen so many turn out to cheer us. This is well intended; we must be indulgent."

Their joy, Michael realized bitterly, suited Lord Santos perfectly; he waved and smiled magnanimously. The icers cheered blindly, and he knew they'd vote for Lord Santos to the man, believing that if he could marry off his niece to an iceman, he must be some fine fellow. It was a kind of promise of better things to come, one Lord Santos would fulfill by squeezing their life's blood to line his pocket.

"Long live Michael!"

"Long live Jacinta!"

The distant echoes of the chant could be heard even as they lifted above the basin to strike toward Castle Santos.

When the wedding party disembarked, the guests were already waiting on the terraces and in the atrium where feasts had been laid. The starborn had speedily flown over the tundra, unconcerned with the icer rabble thronging the road, eager to be at resplendent Castle Santos, where visitors were rare. Even Lord Santos's own entourage from the Consortium and the security forces had been honored with invitations; the halls were filled with starborn gentry.

Michael noticed an increase of castle guards. They were evident everywhere. Even though no one could enter without an invitation, Lord Santos would realize he was especially vulnerable this day. He could not screen every guest with the care he used in smaller settings. Michael wondered if he suspected treachery from his own handpicked guests.

There was no hope for even a moment alone with Jacinta. Michael hadn't expected any while the starborn made up for their somber assemblage at the chapel with boisterous celebration, which seemed to consist mostly of drinking and dancing. When Jacinta was whisked away from him for the dozenth time for yet another dance with a starborn man, the crowd around Michael tactlessly dispersed, as it had each time Jacinta left his side. The starborn still wanted no truck with an icer. Michael carefully noted that Lord Santos and Cosimo were deeply involved with guests, then he ducked into the family wing, confident he wouldn't be missed.

There were guards here, too, but only in the corridors. He passed through Lord Santos's study and stood in the empty hallway listening for any sound from a lingering servant. He passed a silent count of one hundred, then with stealth darted into the pantry and down the plasteel stairwell, not allowing his boots to make a sound. Below the permafrost was the stone staircase, and below that the drop shaft.

The drop shaft was lifeless, the energizer unresponsive to his palm. He hadn't really expected it to respond. He looked down; the gangplank landing was empty, the only sound was the low hum of the kettles. From under his tunic, Michael withdrew a slender coil of rope and swiftly fastened one end to the rail at the stair. After another cautious look through the shaft, he dropped the rope to the planking. Hand over hand he lowered himself, watching all the while for a technician to appear.

Once on the landing, he listened again, but there were no telltale footsteps. He was perspiring, wondering where the tech was. Perhaps he had gone to the kitchen for a few moments to partake of the luscious food being prepared for the guests. It wasn't unheard of for a tech to sneak out of the kettle room even on *Ship Lisbon*, but on the ship it was because they could rely on Michael to cover for them. He cursed the sloppy tech, certain now that he would have to seek him out, which would take an undetermined amount of time that he could ill afford to lose.

Still walking quietly, Michael went to the control panel. Above it, the lighted schematic representation of the energy paths glistened with bright green connectors and gates, every drop shaft, lift shaft, pylon, and beam that was reinforced with antigrav architecture. His eyes retraced the path to the tarmac, and when he was certain of the critical junctions, he turned his attention to the control panel. So familiar with the dials and levers was he that his hands moved almost instinctively. He reset them, watching for minute responses on critical dials. He glanced back up at the schematic. When he saw all but the path to the tarmac turn a telltale yellow, he stepped back, satisfied.

"What are you doing!"

Michael whirled to see the tech standing behind him. His concentration on the controls must have prevented him from hearing the tech's approach, but he didn't let surprise interfere with thought now. "You've left on the drop shaft energy, you incompetent fringer!" Michael snarled.

"No," the tech said. Suspicious as he must have been, he glanced at the shaft to check, and in that instant Michael jumped him, stiletto in hand. The tech sagged as the knife ripped his brain. Michael let him drop to the planking, then wiped the blade on the dead man's tunic.

After a recheck of the dials, Michael bounded back to the shaft, the adrenalin pumping through his system making the climb up a quick trip, almost effortless. He coiled the rope and replaced it in his tunic, then hurried up the stairs. He paused a moment to wipe the sweat from his brow and to catch his breath. The corridor was still empty. After a final check for any sign of disarray on his uniform, he walked casually to the door of the family wing. A guard stepped aside smartly, letting him pass, and he stepped into the atrium.

He stood unobtrusively by the wall, watching the dancers sway by in time to the music. It seemed to take forever before he detected a satisfying vibration beneath his feet, a rhythmic sequence for which the dance score could not account. Jacinta saw him and waved, and when the dance ended, she threaded her way to him.

"They'll be kidnapping me soon," she said almost apologetically, "for the bride chase."

"I know." He smiled at her. "Will you lead me a merry chase?"

"No," she said, then laughed when he started to protest. "I'm going straight to our suite at the Consortium to soak my feet. A navigator's feet aren't accustomed to all this dancing."

"I hope it will be over soon," he said.

"It had better be," she said. "If I have to dance with one more Consortium official, my blisters will get blisters."

Lord Santos himself appeared out of nowhere and took Jacinta's hand. She smiled resignedly, and left Michael yet again. Grandly the music resumed, and Michael knew that in minutes the crowd would hustle Jacinta to the tetheryard, where a zepp-carriage awaited the bride, and the chase over the countryside would begin. That is, it would if the groom were lucky enough to escape the restraining crowds and reach his own zepp-craft.

Grateful for enforced anonymity among the starborn, he slipped out of the atrium, intending to use a lift shaft, but Cosimo barred his way.

Cosimo rudely seized Michael, his grip like a vice on Michael's arms. "No easy quarry for you, bridegroom," he said drunkenly. "You've already gained too much, too easily for an iceman. I'm going to make sure you earn your wedding night with a long chase!"

He shoved Michael through a door into a small sitting room. "House monitor, lock the door," he said, and Michael heard the bolts slide into place.

"Cosimo, I . . ."

"Be silent!" Cosimo said, and pushed him back toward a chair. "You're going to sit down and listen quietly while I tell you some things about your sweet new bride. Things a husband ought to know about his wife."

"I'm not interested in anything you have to say," Michael said, pulling out of Cosimo's grasp. "I just want . . ."

A lase-blade appeared in Cosimo's hand, and he jabbed at Michael, missing slicing off his jaw by mere centimeters. Warily, Michael backed away. Cosimo might be drunk and smaller than Michael, but a drunken swipe from a lase-blade was just as deadly as a sober one. Still, he had to get past quickly. Time was already running short.

"Did you really think we'd give you a good Ballendian woman?" He shook his head, bloodshot eyes dilated like black coals. "A pure one?"

"Cosimo, you're drunk. But if you don't let me pass . . ."

"Don't threaten me, you throwback," Cosimo snarled.

"Get out of my way."

"What's the matter, iceman. Don't you want to know that I was the first man to touch her?"

"Not by her will," Michael said. He watched the eyes, not the knife, wanting an opening to bolt for the door. But the man was not that drunk.

"Oh, she squeals a lot when I touch her, but I was never fooled. She loved it. I could see her nipples get hard right through her dress. You think that would happen if she didn't like it?" He laughed, never taking his eyes off Michael. "Now you sit down, throwback, right over there in that chair. Because I have lots more to tell you about your prissy bride. And you're going to listen for a long time. And when I'm sure the bride carriage has a good head start and if I think you've learned what you need to know, maybe I'll let you go." He pushed Michael with his free hand, intending to send him backward into the chair, but Michael grabbed Cosimo's arm and twisted it behind him. Cosimo spun, but he reached over his shoulder with the lase-blade. Michael dodged, twisting the man's other arm higher. Cosimo howled and started bringing the lase-blade from the other direction. The angle was not good, but he would not need to do much more than touch Michael, and his reach was surprising. Michael let him go and jumped out of the way.

"Nearly got your hand, didn't I," Cosimo said. He crouched. "Well let's just see how Jacinta likes being touched by a hand with no fingers." He slashed at Michael, but Michael dodged.

"What's the matter, Cosimo. Are you upset because she never let you touch her at all? Is that it? You want to punish Jacinta for rebuffing you by maiming me? Well, come on, little man. Let's see you try."

Cosimo lunged again, but this time Michael kicked the knife hand and threw himself at Cosimo as he was faltering, pressing the blade into Cosimo's stomach. It sliced through tunic and flesh alike, stunning Cosimo enough so that Michael could push again and plunge again and plunge it higher, the blade ripping through the rib cage to the heart.

Cosimo's eyes bulged in disbelief.

"You stupid banty," Michael said. "You never guessed that I would kill you, did you?" He stepped aside to let Cosimo fall.

"Why?" Cosimo said. He'd gone to his knees, bleeding profusely.

"If I had the time, I'd spend it taking your balls for Jacinta, not telling you why."

Michael shoved him over and stepped past the growing pool of blood. "House monitor, is there anyone in the hall?"

"No. The hall is empty."

"Open the door."

The door slid open, and Michael stepped out. "Now close the door, and don't open it again until tomorrow."

Michael was running for the lift shaft even as the door closed, but he feared he was already too late.

CHAPTER
12

In the atrium, the crowd had surrounded Jacinta and her uncle and then swept them onto the terraces, separating them. When she heard her uncle exchanging lighthearted ribaldry with the men, she stopped even token resistance. He disgusted her, even in his speech, and she quite suddenly realized this could very well be for the last time. Her papers were safe with Michael now. She let herself be urged across the tarmac and into the zepp-carriage. Genuinely weary, she sank back into the comfortable seat, staring at her uncle as he waved to her from the upper terraces. As the zepp-carriage rose and moved to the edge of the tarmac, she saw her uncle going back inside. She felt incredibly relieved. She'd actually done it, and gotten away with it. Her heart started beating wildly, and she couldn't restrain a laugh. She saw the pilot raise his eyes to look at her in the reflection of the heads-up display on the control panel.

"If it weren't for the chase, the bride would surely be danced to death," she said to him. She kicked off her shoes and held them up. He nodded slightly, but didn't seem to share her amusement.

She couldn't help her exhilaration, as much from the celebration as the realization that at last she had obtained freedom to pursue the stars. Nothing could stop her now,

173

not her family, the bloodlaws, not even Michael should he
still be dreaming she might change her mind about not
invoking their right to bond in the Corps. Ensign Jivar,
navigator of the Corps of Means, but not a mere ensign
for long. Starship pilot, officer, even a starship command! .
Nothing was beyond her grasp now, not ever again.

As the zepp-carriage gained altitude and wound around
the castle, she peered at the crowd on the tarmac, realized
that the bridegroom's craft was still securely tethered. It was
mostly servants, icers, waiting to cheer their hero when he
took off after her.

"They probably disabled it," she said idly to the pilot.

"It doesn't matter, Madam Jivar," the pilot said, "he'll
not need it."

At the sound of the pilot's voice, Jacinta sat upright,
alarmed. She leaned forward to look at him. "Hansen?"
she said.

He turned and nodded grimly. His hair was no longer
gray, and he wore Santos livery, but there was no mistaking
that it was Hansen.

The craft pulled sharply back to Castle Santos.

"Why are we turning?" They were supposed to be going
to the Consortium Towers atop Cradle City. But what was
Hansen doing in the pilot's seat? She could think of no good
reason. "Take me to the towers," she demanded sharply.

"We're cut off now from the crowd's view. We're going
back to the other side of the castle to get Michael."

"Michael?" Jacinta said. "He's to follow in the other
craft. What's going on? Is this Michael's way of making
sure I won't disappear for the night?"

"Hush, girl. This will be tricky. If he's not there now,
there'll be no second chance," the iceman said.

She could tell he was tense as he drew the craft level
with the upper battlements. Well he should be! It was
dangerous to maneuver the craft so close to a structure like
Castle Santos. The drafts could dash them against the stone
fences. Frightened, Jacinta held her breath as he skimmed

just above the parapet walk. She could see the guards watching the strange maneuvering of the bride craft, but they merely seemed curious, not alarmed. The craft moved slowly past the first of the big guns, and Hansen cursed.

"Where is he?" Hansen said, looking frantically through the viewplates.

Jacinta saw a shadow, and Hansen hit the switch for the door. Michael hurtled in, sprawling over Jacinta's feet as the door snapped shut.

"Why weren't you at the third gun as we planned?" Hansen said angrily. "Those guards would never have allowed a second pass. As it is, they've probably alerted security."

"I was . . . detained. Cosimo grabbed me as I was leaving," Michael said, still gasping. He turned, but stayed on the floor, below the zepp-carriage's viewplates.

"How'd you get away?"

"I'll tell you later," Michael said, glancing at Jacinta.

"As long as you're all right, Mikey boy," Hansen said.

"Michael, what's going on?" Jacinta said coldly. "Why is Hansen here? How did he get my uncle's livery? What are you doing in the bride craft?"

Michael sat up, glancing out the viewplates, as if to check their altitude, not answering her.

"How soon?" Hansen asked Michael.

"Soon," Michael said. "I could feel the resonance in the floors when I left the battlements. The guards probably could, too, but even if they figure out why, it won't matter."

"What won't matter?" Jacinta said.

Again Michael didn't answer.

She reached over and jerked his lapels to make him look at her, but he just pulled away. His silence frightened her. Something was terribly wrong. The magnitude of a conspiracy that put Hansen in her uncle's livery and in control of one of his craft while she was in it wasn't seeming like a bridegroom's prank to her any longer.

"The servants seem to be out on the tarmac in full force," Hansen said, smiling for the first time.

Michael sat up to look out. He nodded and looked at Jacinta for the first time. "Thank you, Jacinta," he said. "Thank you for asking them to watch the bride chase. Thank you for saving my people's lives."

Again Jacinta tried to grab Michael by the lapels, but again he pushed her hands away. "Michael, what . . ."

"There!" Hansen shouted, cutting her off. "Y' di' it, Mikey boy. Y' di' 't."

Jacinta looked out the viewplates where Hansen was pointing. The now-distant outline of Castle Santos seemed to bulge for a second before what she could only describe as a powerful implosion seemed to suck the walls down into what was once the atrium. When the noise of the holocaust reached them a moment later, the castle was already flattened, only the tier with the tarmac remained, the people there scurrying like ants. Above, Cradle City loomed, a gape of thick dust where Castle Santos used to be.

For a moment, Jacinta could only stare, too stunned to speak. The dark cloud of dust was rising steadily, so thick it obscured Cradle City. Beneath the cloud, she knew there could be nothing but rubble, acres of structural plasteel and stone, among it all the bodies of her uncle, Cosimo, and hundreds of other starborn.

"What have you done?" She turned back to Michael, who would not look at her. She looked at Hansen. "What are you?" she demanded wildly. "This isn't the work of icemen. Are you knaves? Or is this Master Rayks's work; you're his man, Hansen!"

Hansen shook his head. "Master Rayks will not benefit greatly from this havoc, but that's incidental. The icers will benefit."

"Why would even icers deal in carnage like this?"

"There'll be no election when the election committee realizes one of the ambassadorial candidates has been killed and they see the turmoil. They'll investigate. Lord Santos won't be around to throw golddust in their eyes, and this time they will see that things are not as they should be on

Earth. They will report what they find to the Council of Worlds. That's why I'm here."

"To kill my uncle?"

Hansen nodded. "And the Consortium hierarchy. It will take years for the Consortium to recover. The Council of Worlds will have to reevaluate the entire situation here on Earth. Maybe they will even become more involved in what's going on here, stop the pillage."

"Pillage!" she almost shouted. "You murdered hundreds of starborn to save some frozen relics?"

"We didn't expect you to understand," he said. "Unless you've lived under starborn rule, you couldn't possibly understand. What's important to you is that your uncle will not exert any influence on your career in the Corps of Means."

"Don't lay this bloodbath on my shoulders. You didn't do this for me," she said coldly.

Michael finally stirred. "No, not for you. But your papers are safe because of it, and the Earth is, too." He glanced at Hansen. "At least, for a while."

"And you'll hang for it," Jacinta said savagely.

"I'm already dead," Michael said looking back at the still-billowing cloud. "Only the bride's zepp-carriage took off from Castle Santos. Along with a lot of innocent people, the groom perished."

Jacinta realized observers would confirm that. Michael's boarding of the bride craft was unprecedented, and because of the stealth they'd exercised, probably unseen by anyone who'd lived to tell about it.

"And you think I'll keep silent?" she asked impatiently. "Or do you plan to kill me, too?"

Michael shook his head. "You can do as you like. Hansen will take you to Cradle City. Play the part of the tragic bride who was widowed on her wedding day. Your papers are your own. You are free. Go back to the Corps of Means, or do whatever you like." Michael shrugged apathetically.

"Do you really think you can buy my silence with my papers," she said, aghast.

Michael stared at her, his face infuriatingly impassive, his eyes almost dull. "It doesn't matter, Jacinta. Use your head. You can tell them the truth if you wish, but then your marriage will surely be annulled. Who gets your papers then? Anselem?"

Jacinta sat back in the seat, helpless with rage. Anselem! What could the little brat do? Maybe nothing at first, but she couldn't imagine him letting her return to the Corps of Means when it was within his power to stop her.

The zepp-carriage made a wide, sweeping turn, dropping altitude until they were well below the bluffs along the river. Then Hansen gained just enough lift to take the craft into a wide ravine. It was a wilderness area, a glacial tongue spread through. The craft couldn't be seen from the basin, Cradle City, or even from the tundra.

"You used me," she said angrily.

"No more than you were using me," he snapped. "We had a bargain."

"One you dreamed up," she said. "You saw that I felt trapped, and you took advantage of me by offering a deal you knew I couldn't turn down. And you lied to me."

"I didn't lie," he said. "I kept my end of the bargain. You get your papers and you get to keep your precious jacks. That is what you wanted, isn't it? To keep your jacks and return to the Corps free of any family limitations?"

"The lie was in the price I'd have to pay," she said. "My uncle and cousin murdered along with hundreds more, and me carrying the name of the man who killed them. How can you expect me to live with that?"

"The same way you live with the memory of that night of the shuttle crash when you took your clothes off to save your life. In silence."

"Now that must have been a sight," Hansen said.

"Michael!" Jacinta said, appalled. "Is nothing sacred to you? You promised not to tell."

Hansen turned and tossed a cloth bundle to Michael. "Change your clothes," he said, "we'll be at the dropping-off place soon." And through a smile too much like a liar's, he said to Jacinta, "Don't worry, icers don't care what a woman wears, or who sees her without, or even what you do when you're without."

"Just what do you think I did?" she asked Hansen archly. "Because if you think Michael and I . . ."

Michael cut her off. "She found a way to survive a bad situation by taking off her clothes. That's all she did," he said sharply to Hansen. "You or I wouldn't have given it a second thought, but for a Ballendian lady, it was an incredibly brave thing to do. Now will you both just leave it alone? I'm sorry I mentioned it."

"Why did you mention it?" she demanded, and before he could reply, she said, "Or couldn't you resist flaunting the last element of trust between us? You lied to me. You let me trust you. And you betrayed me. And that is the long and the short of it, isn't it?"

"Except for one thing," Michael said.

Jacinta looked at him; there was no reasonable defense. What new lies would he tell now?

"I love you."

She wasn't stunned. She'd guessed as much. "Do you think that makes me feel better?" she said, her voice deliberately icy.

She was pleased to see he couldn't hide his disappointment.

"Mikey," Hansen said. "Change your clothes. We're almost there."

Jacinta looked out, away from Michael, as he dug in the cloth sack. The ravine had narrowed, tall, dark walls loomed on both sides. She stared hard at the walls, trying not to be aware that Michael was only a few feet away, pulling off his uniform tunic. She could see the flesh of his bare arms, and she could feel her neck getting red. She had seen male bodies in flats and holos, but never in the flesh. "Michael, stop!" she said. "You can't get undressed in front of me."

"I'm your husband," he said as he took off one boot.

"In name only," Jacinta gasped, terrified now. She squeezed her eyes shut, waiting for the other boot to fall.

"Hansen, open the luggage compartment," Michael said.

"It's not heated," Hansen said.

"Just open the damn thing," he said.

She heard him pull up the seat, which covered the passenger compartment entry to the luggage compartment. When it dropped shut, she knew Michael was gone, and she opened her eyes.

"He needed only not marry me," Jacinta said bitterly. "My uncle could never have won the election without the wedding."

"The wedding was a bonus. The only question was whether you'd be in the castle when it went or not. This plan has been in the works for years."

"Years!" Jacinta gasped. "But how could you know that my uncle would let Michael visit the palace? We didn't even know each other before . . ." Hansen glanced at her, and it all came to her clearly then. "The shuttle malfunction, those men . . . all planned?"

Hansen nodded. "Architectural drawings don't exist to guide a furtive saboteur to Castle Santos's kettle room. It had to be someone who had freedom to survey from the inside, and who had the training to carry out the sabotage, and lastly, had the motive and intelligence to carry it off. Mikey was born with intelligence, and the motive was reinforced every day of his life. We needed only to provide the technical training and the circumstances so that he could perform."

"The Corps of Means provided the training, but even if you arranged the shuttle crash, you could not know . . ." Her voice drifted off as she thought about so many systems failing at once on the little shuttle. Even the transponder had not worked. "Michael didn't sabotage the shuttle by himself," she said flatly. "How big is this network?"

"Do you think I'd tell you even if I knew?" Hansen asked her.

Jacinta considered. It had to be more than just a handful of disgruntled Earth natives, but how much more? If there was Michael and at least one accomplice aboard *Ship*

Lisbon, did that mean the general population of the starlanes held two in each five hundred? "I told Michael about the kettles because I trusted him," she said. "But he already knew, didn't he? Just as he knew that a blood-debt could be exchanged one way or another to get him into Castle Santos."

"The plan was for him to ask your uncle for assignment to Castle Santos as kettle tender. That would have been less risky than this."

"Terrorists," she said flatly.

"We are patriots," he said firmly. "You starborn have corrupted the 'Merican government with your treaties and trade agreements, promising better conditions. The longer you stay, the worse it gets. Then you even have the gall to send one of your own to represent us in the Council of Worlds. We couldn't let that happen."

"Now you'll have no one," she said. "Is that better?"

"Yes," he said. "Until it's one of ours, none is better."

It was stupid to argue with him; he was a zealot, ignorant and narrow-minded. Still, she felt inadequate even trying to reason with him. She'd never been interested in politics, not even Council of Worlds's politics, let alone Earth's. She wished she'd used her jacks for all those political science courses that had been available to her, and then she cursed herself. Fine time to think of that!

The velvety seat popped up, and Michael climbed back into the passenger compartment. He was wearing homespun woolens and cracked leather boots.

"Don't forget to take your uniform with you," Hansen said.

"I have it," Michael said. He patted the cloth sack, which bulged to the shape of his boots. The sword and scabbard were knotted to the sack with twine.

Outside, the walls of the ravine were low, the ice filling the space between.

"What will you do, Michael?" Jacinta finally asked. She tried to act composed, but she still felt shaken, frightened.

"I'll go back to the ice. A man can disappear in The Cold for a lifetime. I'll be nonexistent," he said with a resentful laugh.

"Just ahead now, Mikey boy," Hansen said, interrupting. "They'll be waiting for you."

Michael nodded, but turned to look at her. Jacinta could see he was disturbed. "I know I brought this on us. And maybe you won't believe me, but I wish it could have been different."

"Different," she said dully. His passive acceptance of what he had just done frightened her.

Michael reached into his tunic and pulled out the cylinder containing Jacinta's papers and handed it to her. "I've left a will in my locker in the ship," he said. "It's been carefully written so that you will have control of your dowry and papers. What you do with them now is in your own hands. Your uncle deserved to die, if only for what he has done to you."

"He didn't deserve to die," Jacinta said.

"Yes, he did." Michael said simply. "He was thoroughly evil. More than any other single person, he was responsible for the starborn rape of Earth. Even you," he said.

"He didn't rape me."

"Are you going to kid yourself into thinking what he did was all right just because he's dead?"

Jacinta sat wordless, stunned to realize that even now she could not forgive her uncle. She didn't regret his death, or even Cosimo's, not after what they'd done to her. But had they deserved to die because of it? She just didn't know.

"If you ever think of me . . ." Michael curbed whatever it was he wanted to say and turned away from her.

"You honestly think I'm not going to tell," she started to say, but at that moment the zepp-carriage hovered just above the ground in a small, wind-cleared opening of desolate rock. Michael opened the door and leaped out.

"Don't be a fool," he said, holding the door. "Don't throw away what has been won for you at high cost." With a final look at Jacinta, he closed the door, turned, and ran quickly for cover of rocks and scrub trees.

Hansen turned the zepp-carriage sharply and went back
the way they had come. Jacinta looked back, but couldn't
see any flash of rust and gray.

"What are you going to do?" Hansen said after they'd
ridden in silence for a long time.

"Are you worried, Hansen?" she asked.

"Yes," he said frankly. "I wouldn't have spared the likes
of you."

Remembering her first meeting with Hansen, Jacinta nodded. "It wasn't just your acceptance Michael was asking for
that day. It was my life."

"Yes."

"And for you to put yours in my hands," Jacinta said,
eyeing him. "But he's gone now. You could kill me and
escape like he did into the tundra. They wouldn't be any
more likely to find you than Michael."

"Banty sticks would never find me, but Michael would.
And he wouldn't give up until he did, and I ask you, what
kind of life would that be? Besides, I gave him my word. I'll
take you to the Consortium Towers, like any proper driver
would."

"If I tell what I know, you'll not be able to escape."

"That's true," Hansen agreed stonily.

Jacinta was overwhelmed with anger and resentment,
but, she realized hotly, not with grief. She might have
killed her uncle and maybe even Cosimo if she thought
she could get away with it, though not for their politics.
Just for touching her the way they did. But wishing them
dead was not the same as really killing them, and being
used by Michael was not much less insidious than their
use of her. Still angry, Jacinta opened the crystal cylinder.
The papers dropped out on her lap, and with them a tiny
band of tarnished metal. She picked up the smooth circle,
curiously turning it.

"His mother's wedding band," Hansen said. "A pledge
of faithfulness."

"To me?" she asked.

"I do not see how you could interpret it any other way," Hansen said unhappily.

"Will you see Michael again?" she asked.

"I don't know," he said.

He was probably telling the truth, she realized. If Hansen were caught, he wouldn't be able to tell where Michael was. "Tell him something for me if you do."

"There's only one thing he'd be glad to hear from you."

Jacinta looked at Hansen. "What's that?"

"That you loved him, even if just a bit," Hansen said.

Strangely, the thought didn't horrify her. She sighed and leaned back in her seat. "Then, tell him that," she said.

Hansen scowled. "It wouldn't cost you anything to actually say the words."

"And it would mean so much to him?" she said, deliberately mocking. She shook her head. "You tell Michael Jivar what you will, if you want to make him feel good. But while you're at it, pray that we never meet again. Because if we do, I'll be ready. No one will ever use me like this again. Especially not Michael Jivar."

Despite her outburst, she realized Hansen was smiling. No doubt he realized he'd get to eat his dinner at home tonight. Damn. She was so transparent! And for her there'd be no respite, not tonight, not soon. She wasn't going to escape the event investigator this time.

The spires of Cradle City were dull with dust, but there they were. She stared at them, trying to steel herself for what she still had to face. But how could she pretend to be nothing more than the innocent bride when she knew so much? Wouldn't the event investigator order a truth probe, and then Anselem . . . *Mindset!* she told herself sternly. Practice weeping. Not even an event investigator would subject a Ballendian bride to anything but a sympathetic interview. Not with her spotless reputation of female Ballendian submissiveness that even Corps reports would uphold. She would be back in Corps rust and gray tomorrow if she could just get through today.

Impatiently she replaced the papers in the cylinder and slipped the ring on her little finger. Just wait until next time, Michael Jivar, she thought. Just wait. But she didn't really believe there'd be a next time. She would return to the starlanes, and he would remain locked in The Cold here on Earth. She would never see Michael again, she realized. At last, Jacinta cried.

CLASSIC SCIENCE FICTION
AND FANTASY